Ragtime
Swing

Love Songs from Deus

Ragtime Swing

4 Horsemen
Publications, Inc.

Lyra R. Saenz

Ragtime Swing
Copyright © 2021 Lyra R. Saenz. All rights reserved.

4 Horsemen
Publications, Inc.

4 Horsemen Publications, Inc.
1497 Main St. Suite 169
Dunedin, FL 34698
4horsemenpublications.com
info@4horsemenpublications.com

Typeset by MC
Edited by JM Paquette

Library of Congress Control Number: 2021951160

Print ISBN: 978-1-64450-413-0
Audio ISBN: 978-1-64450-391-1
Ebook ISBN: 978-1-64450-412-3

Table of Contents

Dedication

To love, in all its forms.

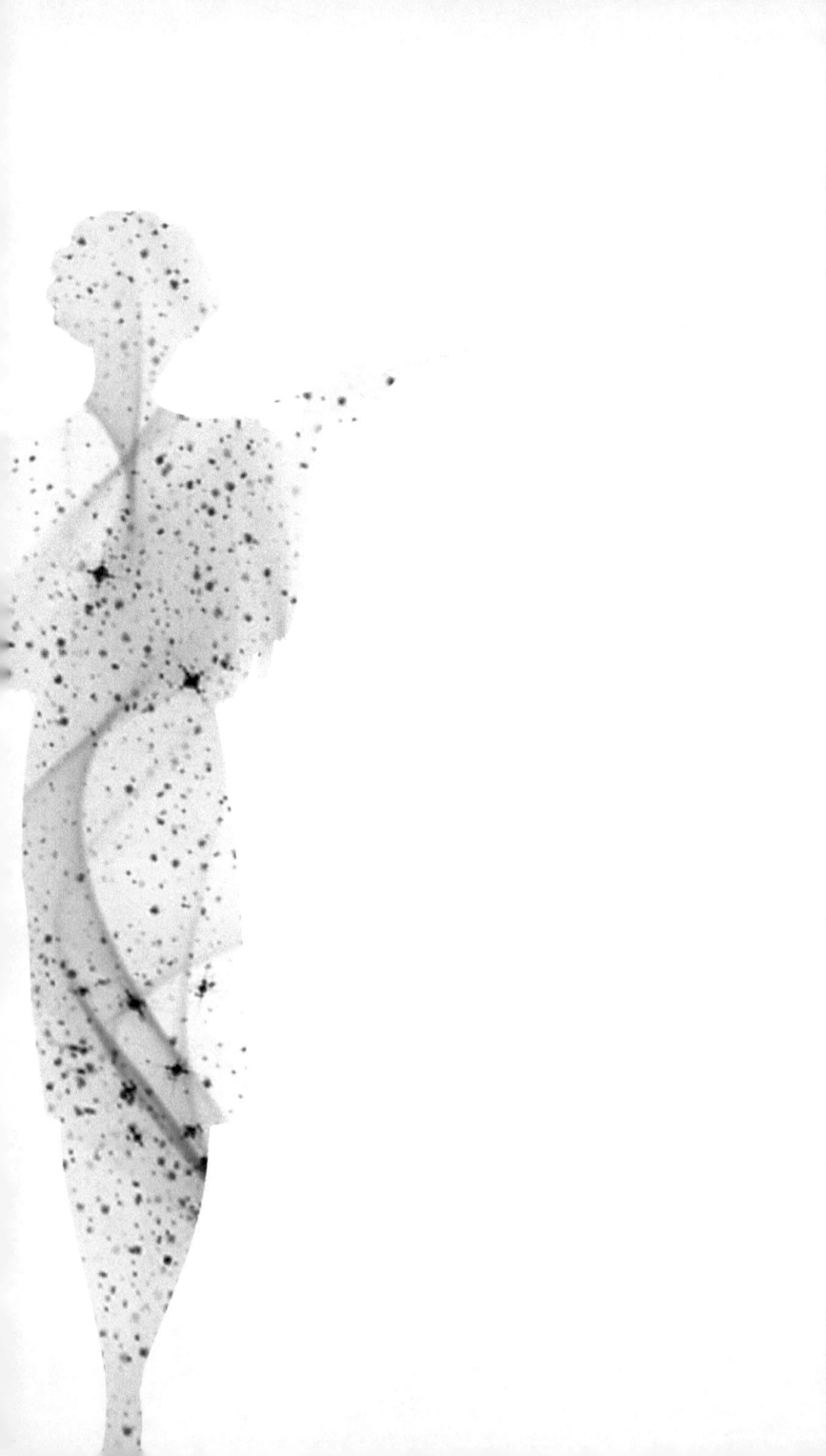

Polyphonic

The trees have kept some lingering sun in their branches,
Veiled like a woman, evoking another time,
The twilight passes, weeping. My fingers climb,
Trembling, provocative, the line of your haunches.
My ingenious fingers wait when they have found
The petal flesh beneath the robe they part.
How curious, complex, the touch, this subtle art—
As the dream of fragrance, the miracle of sound.
I follow slowly the graceful contours of your hips,
The curves of your shoulders, your neck, your unappeased breasts.
In your white voluptuousness my desire rests,
Swooning, refusing itself the kisses of your lips.

"The Touch" by Renée Vivien
An Old World Poem

Ragtime Swing

THE TEARDROP PEARL AROUND HER NECK is warm to the touch and growing warmer as she continues to fiddle with it.

She doesn't know what she's doing here.

Magdalena's comm unit buzzes in her pocket, barely audible over the speakeasy band playing to her left. The trumpet player wails his way through a particularly upbeat solo before colorfully playing his way down the scale to land on a dark downbeat which cues the rest of the band to rejoin. The ensemble of mostly classical instruments (a standing bass, a full drum set, a saxophone, a synthe piano, and of course, the trumpet), when amplified through the venue's sound system, make for a deceptively powerful overture, and the husky tenor of the singer's voice is downright sensual. It all makes the musical tone and texture most fitting for Le Pier Revue, a jazzy nightclub in the heart of central Acapõlco.

Smoke-filled and lit by the naked halogen lights dangling on exposed wires from the ceiling, Le Pier Revue is one of those swanky dives made popular by its "vintage" atmosphere—if bare brick walls, chipped tile floors, and large mosaic windows made of sea-glass could be called vintage, but the bar is clean, the lights aren't glaring, and there are cute mason jars full of sand and seashells acting as centerpieces for the tables surrounding the dance floor. The music is more than palatable, too, none of the cheaply made, deafening electronic stuff most of her students listen to these days.

A dios, she sounds ancient. She's only 28 for crying out loud, yet here she is nostalgic for a time period she never even lived in: anemoia, they call it. Does that make her an anemoiac? Is that even a word? Her husband always calls her an old soul. If it weren't for the charisma enhancer in her head feeding her social cues and tidbits of what the latest trends are, she's sure her students would barely tolerate her. As it is, Adriano keeps telling her she should consider having a beauty enhancer installed. Her darling husband, Adriano Villanueva. It's not because he thinks she's ugly or anything. He suffers chronic annoyance onset by her constantly complaining about how much hair she sheds on a daily basis. Her hair is not as thick as it used to be. She's also been having trouble growing out her nails, and woe be it if she forgets to go without sunscreen one day. Her deep ochre skin will dry out so fast, she'll be slathering on lotion to fight the ashiness for weeks.

Maybe she shouldn't have gone for that doctoral degree. Really, is a piece of paper worth the years shaved off her life by the stress of researching, writing, and delivering a dissertation? That's what her husband asks anyway. Easy for him to say. How was she to know her husband would suddenly hit a gold mine in the second year of their marriage? Three years later, his sudden success, while something she knows she should be thankful for, has made her professorship more of an extracurricular activity than a career, her hard-earned degrees entirely unnecessary to their financial situation. He's living the dream, earning enough for their household alone and arranging things so she can be a pseudo-housewife.

"What can I get you, ma'am?" asks the bartender, a kind dark-skinned college student who may very well be too young to even drink the intoxicating potions he's preparing, but then she remembers the legal drinking age was recently lowered to nineteen in public spaces for private citizens, so okay, he could be old enough to drink.

"Uh, a coconut rum and p-pineapple juice, please."

She hates how she stutters through her usual order. Now she sounds like some underage delinquent trying to sneak a drink, and she isn't surprised at all when—

"Can I scan your ID, ma'am?"

Perhaps, she should take the compliment. It means she looks closer to twenty than thirty, right? She presents her left forearm to him, pointing at the tiny indentation at the crook of her elbow where her ID chip sits just under the skin. His scanner beeps over her arm happily, and a holoscreen unfolds displaying her credentials:

Magdalena Villanueva—Derivan Citizen. ID# 223R986. DOB: 13th Day in the Month of Light 1826.

The bartender's eyes bulge before he catches himself, smiling at her sweetly. *Wow! Does that make her feel old!*

"Would you like to open a tab, ma'am?"

"No, I'll close out," she answers, sliding her credit chip to him.

He nods and sets about making her drink.

And that's the thing, too.

She's supposed to be at home, grading essays. Or maybe, by now, she would be done cooking dinner for herself and her husband, eating her own portion while Adriano's went cold. She should be preparing for bed alone, taking her usual sleeping pill with a full glass of water. Another of Adriano's ideas... She takes them because when her husband slips into bed at three o'clock in the morning, it never fails to disturb her, and once disturbed, she can never go back to sleep. By now, were she at home, she would be setting her system clock to wake her at 7AM, two hours before her first class at the academy so she can go for a morning jog and visit her favorite coffee shop. She should be rolling onto her side and burying her face in a goose-down pillow, reminding herself she loves her husband and should therefore be content because she is well-provided for. His long hours away from home are necessary for his infant fleet, and it isn't like he's gone every day. It only gets like this every three or four months or so. Something about seasonal rushes and shipment planning and extra hours on the boats inspecting the mining operations, but they always last anywhere from two to three weeks when they happen, and they're only halfway through the first week of the cycle and she is so, so lonely.

Perhaps that's why—the loneliness making her act in ways she never actually would.

POLYPHONIC

Because Magdalena is a responsible adult. Not even when she was studying for her degrees did she ever take part in the city nightlife. Okay, there was that one time she played "sober cat" for her best friend's bachelorette party. Her then best friend, anyway. After they got married to their respective partners, they drifted apart. Yet here she is, sitting at the bar of an industrial-themed nightclub that probably sees more tourists than locals on any given night of the year and ordering her favorite drink from a barely legal bartender.

The young man slides her drink across the counter to her. Pretty, in a green-hued sea-glass with deep blue spiral painted into the otherwise clear hurricane glass, the yellow drink almost sparkles in the dim lighting, topped with mint leaves and pineapple slices. The ice in the glass tinkles sweetly as she takes her first sip, and a woman slides into the seat beside her.

"Absinthe, please, if you have it," she orders smoothly.

"We've got it," he responds happily. "Sugar and water with it?"

"Just as is."

"Coming right up."

She can't help but compare her already sweating drink to the woman next to her. Curvy but tall with dirty-blond hair cut in a lovely crimped bob, just long enough on top to tickle her chin but shaved close to the scalp on one side. Her skin is fair and a little rosy from the ever-boiling Derivan sun. She's wearing a glitzy, gold tube dress, patterned with tropical florals. The hem hits her around mid-thigh and pairs surprisingly well with the knee-high combat boots on her feet.

The bartender returns with the mystery woman's drink. She thanks him with a nod, feather earrings bouncing, and fixes her first shot of a green alcohol that almost glows under the lightbulbs.

"They serve absinthe here?"

Magdalena immediately regrets opening her fat mouth because the woman's attention instantaneously shifts from her drink to Magdalena, and wow! She's never seen eyes so pale before.

Those icy blue eyes trace Magdalena up and down, not quite in a predatory way but certainly not in a way that would ever be appropriate outside the confines of a bedroom. She downs her shot in one long draught and exhales the burn, already fixing herself a second serving.

"You don't come here often, do you?"

Heat rises in Magdalena's cheeks, and to keep from sputtering, she takes a long swing of her drink. Predictably, she drinks too fast, and a particularly sour sip of pineapple juice goes down the wrong pipe. Magdalena chokes, turning her face away from the other woman as she coughs the liquid out of her windpipe.

A cool hand pats her gently on the back to help her clear her airway.

"Sorry, I didn't mean to fluster you. You okay?"

"Yes," she coughs out. "Sorry, I drank too fast."

"I can see that," replies the blond, wriggling an eyebrow in the direction of her glass. "You certainly know how to waterfall, don't you?"

Magdalena nearly chokes on her own spit this time. She's nearly downed the entire drink.

"I didn't realize. I—"

The other woman laughs.

"Olga," she offers, holding out a hand.

Magdalena, taken aback by the gesture, takes the offered appendage with embarrassment. "Magdalena."

The blonde hums. "Nice to meet you, Magdalena."

She half expects the woman to butcher the pronunciation of her name. Most foreigners with similarly pale complexions do, unused to the Derivan language and the proper accented parts of words and names, but Olga doesn't. Her name rolls on the woman's tongue as though she is tasting the name, swirling it in her mouth like fine wine looking for the bouquet within the letters. She blushes.

"You can call me 'Lena.' My grandmother used to call me 'Lena' for short."

A long unused nickname, no one has called her "Lena" since she was six years old after her abuelita passed away after a long battle with magic sickness.

She doesn't know why she gives it now, but it seems like the right name to give.

Olga draws back to sip at her drink. The green liquid sloshes in the small glass. And Magdalena has to distract herself from the way the woman's throat works as she swallows lest she embarrass herself further.

"So, what is a beauty like you doing all alone in a place like this?"

So much for trying to avoid embarrassment.

"I don't do this often, or ever really. My—" She cuts herself off from saying the word "husband." After all, she removed her wedding ring before entering the building. "My house gets to be too quiet sometimes, and the band here is nice to listen to."

"Yeah, they're not half bad. They play a nice ragtime swing. It's supposed to be a cover of some new top 30 hit, but I'd be willing to bet my life's earnings they play it better than whatever showpony they have auto-tuned on the original track."

Olga downs the rest of her shot.

"So, you like absinthe?" asks Magdalena.

"It's my favorite drink."

"But it's a witch's drink."

Glossy pink lips quirk upward.

"They do say that, don't they? I wouldn't pay it any mind. The green fairy is not a choosy bedmate. After all, why would they serve it if the only people who drink it shouldn't exist?"

"I guess that's true. I guess. I've never met anyone who favors it."

"Have you ever tried it?"

Magdalena shakes her head.

"Would you like a sip? Most people prefer to fix it with sugar and water, but I like it straight. Keeps it nice and strong."

Magdalena waves her hands.

"Oh, I don't know. I'm not much of a drinker, and I really didn't mean to finish this so fast."

Olga catches Magdalena's hands in her own and holds them before her face, and Magdalena freezes like a bunny caught in a fox's sight.

"You have kind hands," declares the blonde. "Hands that would never hurt someone."

Her thumbs glide over the backs of Magdalena's palms, and one of them slides right down her third finger where her wedding ring would normally sit. Magdalena's eyes, half-lidded and darkly despite their normal honey-gold tone, dilate.

"Do you want to get outta here?"

The bass player plucks a dissonant swing from the lower most octaves of his instrument. The chords resonate bassy and dank, the way Magdalena imagines fat droplets of water would echo in a cave or grotto. Each note dings in the pit of her stomach as Magdalena's dark brown eyes rise to meet the lightest of azuls, and she realizes...

She's never wanted anything more.

2

Bossa Nova

"DO YOU EVER JUST LOOK AT THE STARS *and wonder at how much more of the universe they've seen?"*

The waves lap against the shore, kissing their toes with each cascade inland. Magdalena is still out of breath, still coming down from the incredible high of the other woman's attention on her body. The night air is chilly on the bare skin of her belly and thighs, but Olga keeps her warm. Her curves, soft in all the right places, press into her like a furnace.

Olga's voice flows over her like silk in gentle cadence to the sloshing rolls of the water, and Magdalena looks up at the sky, at the aforementioned celestial bodies twinkling in their own little universes light years away from them. Somewhere up there is the old world. Sol shining at the center of its orbit. She wonders what life is like there. Is it similar to theirs? Or did they destroy themselves the way the hexen believed they would before the old gods helped them build Deus?

"I don't know. I've never really thought about it."

"You'd prefer your books," *laughs Olga.*

"*Books are tangible. I can touch them, and I don't need to put on a space suit to do it.*"

"*Interesting take. I don't think I've ever heard anyone call the stars intangible.*"

"*Well, they are, aren't they? It's not like you could just pluck one out of the sky and give it to someone.*"

"*What if you could?*"

Olga's eyes seem to glow in the light of the little glow light Magdalena carries on her key ring for nights along the beach just like this. She used to enjoy walks on the shore with Adriano when they were younger, more carefree, when Adriano's concerns weren't more focused on money than her.

"*What? Like with magic?*"

Olga shrugs. "Or with science. Whichever you prefer."

"*I don't know. You would get burned, wouldn't you, touching something like that?*"

"*Perhaps. But isn't that the foundation of all passions and adventures? The risk of being burned.*"

26th Day in the Month of Soil, 1854 A.P.–
Acapõlco, Deriva

Two days since Magdalena's visit to Le Pier Revue and still her dreams are haunted by a Valkyrian beauty. Her lips, the silky smoothness of her hair, her fingertips as they ghosted over her skin, the salty taste of her sweat, her gasped sighs. They haunt her in her day-to-day life as she is reading a book or taking her morning jog.

They follow her even into her marital bed, Adriano's attentions lackluster in the wake of a woman's touch.

It's not guilt. She expected guilt. She was unfaithful. She committed adultery, the letter 'A' sewn into her clothes. She violated the sanctity of their marriage vows. She should feel terrible, but she doesn't.

Instead, she yearns.

Her husband comes home early. He swoops into the kitchen as she is preparing to cook dinner and tugs her into a kiss. The burner clicks off. His hands, weather beaten and rough, find their place low on her hips, and he pulls her into an uncoordinated salsa. It's clunky, bearing little sense of rhythm, but he spins her with a teenager's enthusiasm, dipping her for a finish that has her giggling the way she did at their modest wedding reception after one too many glasses of champagne.

"What in the world are you so happy about?" she says through a surprised laugh.

"*Mi amor*, come here."

Adriano pulls her by the hand to their bedroom. On the bed is a lovely, wrapped garment box. A gift for her.

Magdalena panics. What day is it? Did she forget an anniversary again? No. They got married in the Month of Frost.

Adriano hovers behind her, kissing the space behind her ear.

"I hope you like it."

Magdalena's hands shake as she unravels the silk ribbons tying the box together. The lid comes off with a slide of cardboard. She pulls aside the hot pink tissue wrapping paper to reveal a brand new, sparkling ball gown. Unlike anything Magdalena has ever worn before, the gown is made from layers of taffeta cloth, meticulously dyed in an ombre cascade of dark to light shades of blue with a structured bodice embroidered with hundreds of shiny crystals.

"I had it made just for you. It should fit perfectly."

Her mouth gaps like a fish as she holds the extravagant piece in front of her.

"Do you like it?"

"It-it's beautiful, Adriano, but," she hesitates, "what's the occasion?"

"Ay, Magda, don't tell me you forgot. The Seafarer's Ball is tonight. Remember?"

"The Seafarer's Ball?"

"Yes. We have an invitation from the Vulcan of Deriva himself!"

And it hits her. The Seafarer's Ball!!

For his Silver Jubilee, Vulcan Tlanextli is taking a tour of the Derivan isles, hosting evening parties and festivals for the people who are the backbone of his country. This week brings him to Acapōlco, and the Seafarer's Ball is the first in a slew of special events to be hosted for their city. The Seafarer's Ball is just as the name implies, a ball held to honor the seafaring men and women of the Acapōlcan fishing and deep-sea mining fleets. Fleet owners, independent captains honored for their years of service, and the boatmasters who keep the port traffic flowing as readily as the tides themselves. Adriano would be the youngest man in attendance. Despite being a relatively new fleet owner, Adriano received the invitation two months ago and he'd been over the moons about it.

"An invitation from the Vulcan himself! Magdalena, can you imagine? Sharing drinks with the highest members of our society!"

And she could kick herself for forgetting because now she has less than two hours to clean herself up enough to merit wearing this dress.

"Oh, I'm sorry, honey. I completely forgot."

Adriano shakes his head with a chuckle. "That's alright. I knew you would. That's why I came home early."

And he turns away from her, already moving to claim the bathroom for himself.

She wants to get angry at the low jibe, but he is right. She did forget.

With a sigh, she notices for the first time the finely pressed tuxedo hanging from the closet door, the freshly shined shoes below, a pair of gleaming heels, and a clutch to match the lavish dress in front of her.

Bossa Nova

How much did all of this cost? Does it even matter?

A few hours later, Magdalena finds herself sipping champagne and brushing elbows with some of the richest people in Acapōlco on the Vulcan's very own royal yacht. The ship is decorated to the nines. Strings of fairy lights and lanterns made from blue sea glass light the deck. The Derivan flag, light blue with the coral crest at the center, flies proudly from the main mast. There are Moctezumo trainees drifting about the deck passing out hors d'oeuvres and champagne. The band plays a soul-soothing jazz, the kind of music that provides a relaxed background lull, encouraging conversation to flow as easily as the notes themselves.

And the people in attendance are equally glittering. There are various adepts scattered about chatting with the local business and company owners. A gaggle of rich fish wives titter on the edges of the dancefloor. The mayor and his wife gab with Fabian and his sweet-faced partner. Fabian is Acapōlco's sole technomancer, an elderly chap nearing retirement age, whose augmentations are beginning to stiffen with age and battle. He's been in need of an upgrade for years but insists the old equipment is far superior to all that new, fancy tech the young'uns are getting nowadays.

At least the dress fits her perfectly, making her a neat addition to the decor, even if she feels like a fraud wearing it. The hem hits just under her kneecaps, the bodice hugs her barely there curves in a way that the illusion of an hourglass figure shines through, and yes, that is her cleavage. She didn't realize she even had any before this dress.

Adriano positively preened upon seeing her in it. He gave himself a congratulatory pat on the back, saying he knew he had a good eye for color, then promptly ran his hands down her sides. Probably already thinking about taking it off of her. Her husband has always been attentive to details—it's the reason he's seen so much success, and he did indeed do an excellent job of picking a wardrobe for her, but couldn't he have at least asked her input on color choice? Not that she minds navy blue, but she's always preferred the way gemstone colors highlight her café latte complexion. Darker colors just make her feel sad.

"Oh, Magdalena, I absolutely adore your gown."

Magdalena turns to find Lucretia Boleria smiling at her. Thank heavens! Someone she knows, even if only through her husband. Lucretia had been the one to double down on Adriano's business expenses, loaning him the assets he needed to establish himself properly.

"Thank you, but yours is absolutely stunning."

And it is. Lucretia's tawny skin tone glows golden in a dark burgundy gown that fits her like a glove. That's what a real hourglass figure looks like. Her dyed blonde hair swept up in a fancy weave of knots and curls, Lucretia is a woman who looks like she belongs in high society. Not like Magdalena playing pretend.

"Nonsense. You're gorgeous, and I'm so glad to see the filtration system is doing its job. Wúxíng, isn't it?"

Wúxíng Syndrome—a condition caused by exposure to magical radiation. Not an uncommon ailment for people living in the more rural parts of Deriva where Magdalena once lived with her grandmother. Outside the cities, magic lives rich and wild in the sand, soil, and sea, uninterrupted by industrialization. Most cases of magic sickness are negligible and easily managed with medication, but some cases result in Wúxíng, a chronic condition where magical energy builds up uncontrollably in the body. It behaves similarly to the way radiation exposure can lead to certain cancers, but uncontrollable cellular replication is far easier to treat than uncontrollable magic generation.

"Adriano told you about my condition?"

"Oh, yes. He was asking me if I knew any treatment specialists, so I recommended him to this doctor out of Seraphim who specializes in magical maladies, but I don't remember the name anymore. Your augmentations were designed by him, I believe."

"Oh... He didn't tell me that."

"Such an unfortunate condition to have," Lucretia continues as though she hadn't even spoken. "It's a pity you weren't born in the city. Perhaps you could have avoided the magical radiation entirely. Now where is your husband, and how could he dare let his beautiful wife out of his sight?"

"I think he went to get us some champagne."

"How gentlemanly of him. Well, I do hope that I can speak with him. It's about our recent mutual investment."

Recent mutual investment?

"Oh, Adriano hasn't mentioned any investments as of late."

Lucretia seems surprised by this. "I thought you knew. He said he told you everything. My fault. Don't think anything of it. Just a little something that should allow us to pay our workers better. I just need to finalize arrangements with Adriano."

Just then her husband arrives with a pair of champagne flutes in hand. "Here you are darling. Ah, Lucretia. Looking lovely as usual."

"Flatterer." The woman giggles behind her hand and smacks Magdalena's husband on the arm.

"I was just telling Magda about—"

"Ladies and gentlemen," a voice booms over the speakers. "Please direct your attention to the balcony as we give respect to our sovereign, His Royal Majesty, the Vulcan of Deriva, Tlanextli Moctezumo."

There is applause as Tlanextli himself appears on the balcony thrust. The Vulcan is as handsome in person as his photographs portray: salt and pepper hair, a fit frame, and a healthy russet skin tone. Wearing a perfectly tailored tuxedo, the only glimpse she has of his augmentations is the odd glint of his left eye, made of glass and hooked into visual augmentations after an encounter with a sea monster lost him the original. A faint scar marks the injury. At fifty-something, she would hardly think him any different from her own father, but this is a man who has reigned for 25 years not just as the sovereign of Deriva but as a technomancer of the League, one of Deus's distinguished posthuman warriors dedicated to protecting people like Magdalena from the horrors of the supernatural realm. This is a man who is not just a monarch but a highly trained soldier, a man of excellence in both combat and learning. A man whose weapon, a gold-plated spear named Ah-Puch, has cut down the most dangerous of monsters. A technologically integrated superhuman worthy of respect and all the honor he has been awarded.

"My dear compatriots," begins the Vulcan, addressing the party. His voice is soothing like a father accustomed to addressing his children. "It is my honor to stand before you not as a monarch but as a Derivan. When I was a boy, my father took me on my first fishing trip..."

As the Vulcan speaks, Magdalena looks to the people surrounding the man.

On either side of the Vulcan are two women dressed simply but elegantly in the colors of the royal family: ocean blues, purples, and greens. One of them, darker skinned, older than her counterpart and obviously Derivan, stands taller, dignified, her own augmentations on display for the partygoers below. At her hip rests a tetoanea, a shark's tooth sword, a traditional island weapon made from mangrove root and shark teeth, but this is a technomancer weapon, constructed from sea glass and metal instead of the traditional materials and inlaid with energy stabilizing gems to fortify it in combat against magic. There is a coin in Magdalena's purse with this woman's face on it: the Vulcana, Elisabeta, Tlanextli's first wife and the mother of Princess Atzi and Prince Xipilli.

BOSSA NOVA

The other woman is clearly a foreigner, pale-skinned and fair haired. In her hands rests Ah-Puch, the Vulcan's weapon for safekeeping. While she is not as severe a presence as the woman opposite her on the balcony, she is just as entrancing, a person capable of demanding the attention of a room without speaking a single word. She stands with an effortless grace and regality that has nothing to do with the tiara that sparkles from her hair and everything to do with the surety in her posture. And it is not lost on Magdalena that though the gems she wears are not as defining as Elisabeta's, they are gems that could only be worn by a consort to the crown of Deriva. There is only one person this woman could be: the Vulcan's Firefly, Freya Nocturne, a woman who captured the Vulcan's heart so thoroughly he married her despite their difference in station and the ire of his queen. Magdalena knew the Vulcan had a second wife. Who didn't know about the man's decision to marry a woman ten years his junior to the disdain of his first wife? But to parade her in public like this! She never expected he would have her situated so openly at his side.

It must be true then, how deep his love must run for her. Why else would he show her such respect when most of his people tried to forget she even exists?

"...it is in the hearts of the men and women on this ship today that Deriva lives. Your strength, your determination, your perseverance in the face of the churning tides of the sea are what keep this country afloat..."

Behind the two women are a pair of children. The two are Elisabeta's boy and girl, the prince and princess of Deriva and Tlanextli's formal heirs. His eldest, Princess Atzi, now well into her teenage years, stands demurely by her mother, tall and willowy like a weeping flower. The princess is dressed in a simple but elegant floral-patterned gown, her hair done up in a simple knot and the jewels of a princess adorning her head.

Behind Princess Atzi must be Prince Xipilli, still boyish at his age and shorter than his sister. Dressed to match his father, the boy wears a sharply tailored tuxedo, but instead of the blue accents of Tlanextli's vest and tie, the prince seems to be wearing a bright pink bow tie with his blue vest. It is an odd color combination, one that he doesn't seem too happy about if the way he keeps messing with it is an indication. The young prince keeps looking around, fidgety and nervous. He shuffles from one foot to the other, nearly giving his back to the audience before his big sister chides him to be still with a smile.

Magdalena's chest aches at the sight. She'd always wanted a big family. She herself was an only child, and with her parents gone, Adriano is the only family she has left. They've been trying now for more than two years to no effect, and she's beginning to wonder if the fertility treatments are even working.

She acknowledges somewhere in the back of her mind that it's a good thing she chose to dally with a woman rather than another man. The sick builds in her stomach, and she takes a sip of champagne to force the nausea down.

"It is with great honor that my family and I can welcome you in our midst this evening. My son and heir has already begun his training as a sailor and adept. My pride in him is as boundless as the Pacificum herself. Meanwhile, my two daughters grow more beautiful every day—"

Two daughters?

"—like precious gems unearthed from the deepest depths of the ocean. Their growing beauty only matched by their hard-practiced talents and keen minds."

That's right! His Majesty has three children, the youngest of which is Freya's daughter and not much younger than her older brother. Though for the life of her, she can't remember the girl's name. And where is the girl anyway?

Magdalena cranes her neck to the side to see if maybe the girl is tucked behind her siblings or mother, but the space is left vacant as though someone should be standing there. *Well, where is she? Is she ill? Why is she not on the balcony with her mother?*

Perhaps putting the Vulcan's lovechild on display is a step too far?

While there had been a formal announcement of her birth, the girl was not given the title of a princess, and photographs of her have never been released to the public. Rumored to be Tlanextli's favored child even if she is not in the direct line of succession, there had been a slew of scandalous talk when she was born. People who refused to recognize Freya as a true wife to the Vulcan called the girl a bastard—"The Vulcan's shame"—a despicable rumor mill run by the gossip mongers. But Magdalena avoids such things like the plague anyway. She suspects the reason for the girl being kept out of the limelight is far more maternal love than paternal shame. It is said Freya Nocturne is nothing but protective of her daughter, using her husband's sway to keep her daughter's name and face out of the public eye as much as possible. While that won't keep the gossip columns from writing plenty on the young lady and her mother, the little that is printed is sanitized of details and photographs.

Freya seems unconcerned by her missing progeny, and now that she thinks on it, perhaps his missing sister is the reason Xipilli can't seem to stand still.

But then the Vulcan's speech is over, the band striking up loud and raucous with the slide of a trombone.

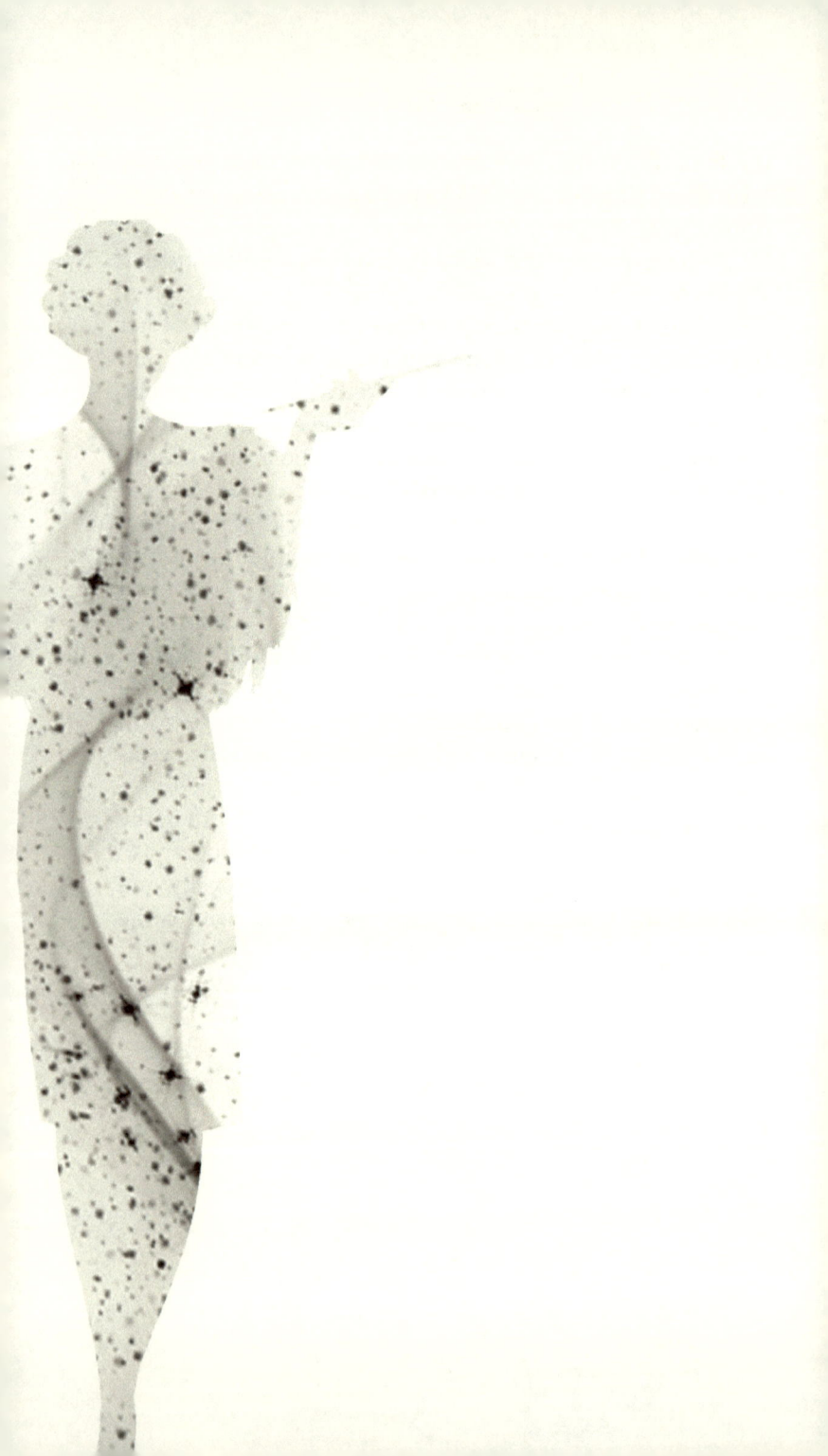

3

A Little Night Music

THE CROWD DISPERSES. SOME PEOPLE move onto the dance floor. Others return to excitable conversation. Most turn in anticipation of the Vulcan and his family making their way into their midst. At her side, Adriano is one of them, giving her a hushed explanation of where he is going and not to move because he'll be right back.

Magdalena takes a moment, all but invisible to the people around her, and watches. She watches them clamor for the monarch's attention. As her husband shoves his way past a lovely couple to get into the cue of people waiting patiently to greet them, Magdalena can't help but feel more than a little spiteful that he told her to wait here, shunning her into a lonely corner rather than have her go with him to offer a bow to Deriva's Vulcan.

The Vulcan escorts the Vulcana onto the deck to a resounding greeting. The two look as regal and powerful as one would expect with Princess Atzi and Prince Xipilli on either side of them, but Magdalena can't help but notice the absence of the Firefly and her daughter. She wonders if Freya would feel shunned by her husband as well for greeting their guests without her or if she chose to abstain from the formal greetings.

It's all suddenly too much, and Magdalena races away from the main deck toward the darker starboard side of the ship. She reaches the banister and heaves over the railing. Her champagne flute shatters on the edge of the deck. The leftover liquid spills across the shiny new shoes purchased special by her husband to go with the dress.

"Are you alright, Señora? Should I call for someone?"

Magdalena whirls around to see a little girl, probably somewhere between nine and ten years old, looking at her with concern. The girl is pretty. Her curly black hair spills in ringlets around her head from the twin pigtails on either side of her head. A tiny tiara is woven into the locks at her crown, fitting for a child her age. She is wearing a simple green formal dress that is more tulle than satin. The gauzy skirt floats from her body like a fairytale and ends right at her ankles to reveal silver sandals. What is a child doing here?

"I'm alright. It's okay. You don't need to call anyone."

"Are you sure? I can tell my dad."

"No need to trouble your father, dearie. I'll be fine in just a moment."

The girl nods.

"My mother gets like that, too. She says it's because she's not an islander like me. She's not a great swimmer either, and no matter how many times my father asks, she refuses to get augmentations, but my brother and I have had ours since we were five. When she goes onboard a ship, she always mixes some ginger with lemon water to stave off seasickness. Always brings her personal mix too even though dad makes sure it gets packed for her with everything else when we go seafaring."

Magdalena smiles.

"It sounds like your father cares a great deal for her."

The girl beams.

"He does. She takes care of him, too. He once got food poisoning from a batch of shellfish that had gone bad. Couldn't get out of bed the next day. He had such bad gas, they had to air out the room twice. Even the doctors wore nose filters to treat him, but she stayed with him, nursing him back to health sans nose filter because she hates putting things on her face, and he was alright in the end."

Well, that's a little too much information, but that's just what you get with children.

"I'm Wren, by the way. I didn't mean to startle you." The girl holds her hand out to Magdalena, and Magdalena takes it. Albeit, she feels a tad awkward shaking the hand of a child.

"I'm Magdalena. Magdalena Villanueva. My husband is waiting to greet Vulcan Tlanextli. Where are your parents?"

The girl giggles. "They're at the party."

At the party? Were people allowed to bring their children to this? Magdalena doesn't recall, but of course, she wouldn't have needed to ask such a question.

"Shouldn't you be with them?"

"Yeah, but I wanted to take a walk around the ship. My brother was making fun of my dress, and my stepmother is in a bit of a foul mood. Figured I'd let her cool down a bit."

Stepmother? This girl has a mother and a stepmother?

"Who are your parents exactly?"

A voice calls to the girl from the path leading to the party.

"Wren, sweetheart, your papa and I were looking for you before the welcome speech. Where did you go?"

When Freya Nocturne, the Vulcan's second wife, rounds the corner, Magdalena nearly heaves again. She's been speaking to the Vulcan's youngest daughter, Wren Nocturne. His youngest daughter who has just revealed to her that apparently his majesty has very bad gas when suffering from an upset stomach.

Wren bounds over to her mother with a skip in her step. "Sorry, Mama, but Sra. Villanueva was ill."

"Oh, and is Sra. Villanueva in need of a doctor?"

"Oh, no, ma'am. That's not necessary," answers Magdalena. "It's just a bit of seasickness."

"Seasickness?" The woman laughs with bemusement. "Here I thought I was the only one on this ship prone to such an ailment."

Her daughter, apparently bored now that the adults are conversing, sashays away to twirl in the light of a string of amber glowing bulbs. Her dress flows around her like gossamer petals, and she hums a strange little cadence in juxtaposition to the bossa nova currently being played by the band at the main party.

"Well, I suppose it isn't just seasickness. This is my first time at an event like this and my husband... well. He's a businessman eager to make new connections, and I'm... well, I teach literature at the local academy."

"An honorable profession. You've nothing to be ashamed of in that."

"That's kind of you to say, but I'd much rather be between the pages of a book than drinking champagne in a pair of heels that have already left blisters on my feet. But I'm here to support my husband, right?"

Freya hums in understanding.

"It took me a while, too. These parties are exhausting at the best of times. I often need to sneak away halfway through for a breather. Normally, I'm content to stay at home for these things. Our Vulcana prefers it that way as well, but Tlanextli insisted I come on this tour. It's his Silver Jubilee after all, and the children are all old enough to enjoy it, and he wanted all of his family here with him even if my own daughter doesn't seem to know where the balcony is for a formal welcome."

The woman's voice raises to emphasize the indirect scolding as she looks over at the dancing girl, but Freya's eyes are soft as she watches her daughter twirl under the fairy lights.

"Your daughter is quite the character," says Magdalena

The woman smiles.

"Wren has all of the stubborn nature of my people with the free-spiritedness of an islander."

"Your people?"

Freya looks to Magdalena, and for a moment, Magdalena could swear that the woman's eyes glimmer like a cat's in the dark, but when she blinks in surprise, the shine is gone, replaced by clear blue-green irises.

"Northerners, I suppose. My family traveled a lot when I was a child, so I couldn't tell you where any of us were actually from, but it was cold most of the year."

"But if you traveled so much, wouldn't that make your people free-spirited rather than stubborn?"

"You would think that, but no. The reason we traveled so much was because we didn't want anyone to own us. It's a tricky thing to wrap your head around. Mostly because people find it terribly romantic to be able to up and leave at the drop of a hat. Some people call it wanderlust. But when the need to move comes not from a desire for freedom but from a fear of being caged, the sentiment loses its romanticism. When you stay in one place for too long, the place claims ownership of you. Makes you a part of the foundations and the root system. Stay in one place long enough and you forget you ever had the freedom to leave in the first place."

"But you stay with the Vulcan?"

Freya smiles. "I do."

"Why?"

The word leaves her mouth without a thought, and Magdalena kicks herself for how improper such a question is. *Asking the Vulcan's second wife why she stays with her husband! Is she mad?*

"I'm sorry. That was rude of me to ask. It's clearly none of my business."

Magdalena's face is on fire, and she gets up to bow or curtsy or something. Freya may not be a queen, but she is married to royalty which makes her the next best thing, right? Magdalena should be prostrating herself on the floor for her flapping tongue. But Freya Nocturne simply laughs, stopping Magdalena from face planting into the ground.

"It's alright. It's a fair question."

"One that you have no reason to answer, your grace."

"Perhaps, but I'll answer it anyway. No need for titles, dearie."

The wind rustles through Freya's hair. It shimmers like starlight under the glow of the moons.

"Even the most stubborn hearts may yield to love. Even the most free-spirited of birds will seek comfort in a nest they can build with their lovers. That is the real power of love, you see. Not that it brings us joy or pleasure or laughter. It gives us all of those things, sure, just as much as it brings us pain and sadness and anger. But more than any trivial emotion love can provide us, true love comes with safety. The safety of home, the safety of trust, the safety of knowing you are not alone. That you will never be alone even if you are leagues apart because there will always be someone looking up at the stars thinking of you as you too gaze up at the sky and think of them. That's what love does for people, and a force that powerful could move even the most stubborn wanderer into standing still.

"That's why I stay. Because Tlanextli took my offered heart and pledged to keep it safe, and I did the same in return. My Wren was born from that love, and she is the most precious gift I could have ever asked for."

And as Magdalena watches Freya watching her daughter, she can't help but feel the same shock that had her leaning over the railing in the first place. But something about the other woman's presence keeps the nausea at bay. It's soothing, putting her at ease, and she thinks she understands why people say she is a soothsayer—an enchantress who seduced her way into a monarch's bed and anchored herself there with a daughter. The rumors even go so far as to claim the little girl's very existence is the product of a love spell.

A Little Night Music

But speaking with Freya, Magdalena now knows that nothing could be further from the truth. Freya Nocturne is a woman in love, and Wren is the product of a marriage overflowing with it.

And that Magdalena is here to bear witness to this woman's heart. It's, well, it's astonishing really.

Magdalena is a nobody. This party is for the fleet owners of Acapōlco's fishing and deep-sea mining corporations, people as necessary to Deriva's infrastructure as the islands themselves, and her husband has carved a path up the ranks to sit among them. She is now just a wife meant to hang off her husband's arm like a trophy even though she's a literature professor at the local academy. She teaches the future generation. Some of her students may even go on to become League certified adepts, maybe even technomancers, joining Deriva's most elite members of society, answerable only to the Vulcan of Deriva, who is himself a decorated technomancer.

Adriano eats it up. This is his first time attending such a prestigious event. Even though his company is barely two years old, he's established himself in this world, possessing a big enough piece of the pie to merit an invitation while she is still just Magdalena, academy literature professor, a woman who married a fisherman and worked herself through her doctoral degree. She doesn't belong here, immersed in high society like a would-be debutante, wearing a gown that may have been made for her but seems to be wearing her more than she is wearing it.

Yet here she stands, sharing the same space as Freya Nocturne, second wife to the Vulcan himself, having a conversation with the woman about love and family and home as though they were anything alike while Freya's young daughter, a girl who is all but a princess of Deriva, sings a mermaid song and dances across the deck. The woman is alluring and beautiful, far more than any photographs or projections of her could possibly do justice. In the moonlight, her pale complexion seems to glow. In the magic of the night, a gossamer of stars blanket her skin. A mysterious magnetism calls to Magdalena like a silent nocturne on a moonlit eve. How appropriate for a woman whose surname is Nocturne.

"Do you have any children of your own?"

Magdalena shakes her head.

"Oh no. My husband and I don't have any children yet."

"Do you want them?"

"Yes, we've been trying, unsuccessfully. I've always wanted a big family, but maybe it just isn't meant to be."

"They will come. Usually at the most unexpected time. Wren wasn't a surprise per se, but I'd never made a goal for myself to have children."

"Most Fireflies don't have children."

It's an acknowledged fact. Not to say Fireflies couldn't have children or anything like that, but having a child around certainly makes the glamour of paying for someone's company in any capacity seem less glamorous.

Freya shakes her head in agreement.

"No, we don't. It makes travel and being a companion difficult, and we don't typically marry kings either."

Magdalena's jaw goes slack as the woman sets her full gaze on Magdalena. Freya Nocturne's eyes are like sparkling, blue-flecked emeralds in the dark. She's never seen eyes that particular shade of aquarium blue-green outside of plastic surgery clinics or colored contact lens brochures. It reminds her of the coral reefs that surround Deriva: crystal clear blue waters colored by green sea grasses and a kaleidoscope of coral reefs and underwater rainbows full of life and rhythm. That's what Freya's eyes remind her of—the beauty of the untouched ocean.

"Your-Your grace, his majesty is looking for you."

Freya looks over to the young Moctezumo trainee making his way to them. The youth is harried as though he has been looking for her for a good while.

"Oh, Quetzal, you know Tlanextli worries too much. There's no need to get in a tizzy about little ol' me."

"My lady, please."

"Alright, alright, you win. Wren, sweetheart, it's time to go back. No more skipping events."

The little girl pouts. "Do we have to?"

"Yes. Now, come along. We have guests to greet. "

"You know Elisabeta doesn't want us there."

"Perhaps, but your father wants us there, and your brother and sister were looking for you all during the welcome speech."

The girl makes a face.

"Xipilli's still bitter I knocked him out of bounds in training yesterday. He keeps saying my dress looks like a jellyfish."

"Well, then be like a jellyfish and give him a good sting in the kidney. Your brother could use a good shock, and I doubt even your stepmother will scold you for catching him off guard. She's been trying to get him to stop slouching for months now, and if he makes a fuss about it, he'll just earn himself extra circuits around the deck tomorrow morning from Quetzal here. Won't he, Quetzal?"

Freya winks at the teenage adept.

"Of course, señora."

"See," Freya tells her daughter, but Wren just makes a face.

"Then he'll just be mad at me for getting him in trouble again."

"Well, then maybe he'll learn not to invite trouble by teasing my songbird."

She bops her daughter on the nose, and the little girl goes cross-eyed for a bit. Magdalena hides a laugh behind her hand. Ah, the wonders of sibling rivalry. The pair share a few more hushed words before Wren turns to her with a curtsy.

"It was nice to meet you, Sra. Villanueva."

Magdalena gives her own awkward curtsy in return.

"You as well, young lady."

Freya sets a hand on Wren's shoulder.

"We'd best return to the party. It was lovely chatting with you Mrs. Villanueva."

Magdalena bows deeply.

"You as well, ma'am. Thank you for keeping me company."

"Ah, but it is I who should thank you. Enjoy the rest of your evening." The pair turn away from her, heading down the deck, but just before they are out of sight, Freya looks over her shoulder at Magdalena. "Oh, and do be mindful to avoid the champagne or any other alcohols for a few days."

"I—I'll do that, ma'am."

Freya Nocturne and her daughter disappear into the glitter of the party, and even though she is once again alone, Magdalena feels a little less lonely. After all, who could feel lonely when the wife of a Vulcan has shared with you something that no mortal man or woman should ever know?

4

Crescendo

MAGDALENA LETS HER HUSBAND KNOW she is feeling unwell, and Adriano's eyes close at her desire to leave the party early. Not that he isn't concerned about her wellbeing, but this is a huge networking event for him. One that will not come again for another 25 years. So, she reassures him that she can make her own way home and not to worry. She'll just call herself a Ryde. They came in one anyway. It's cheaper than a taxi, and they knew there would be alcohol at the event and neither of them have filtering systems as part of their augmentations, and besides, they can afford an extra fare, right?

The relief in his expression almost hurts her feelings, but it's a hollow moment, one brought on by an already established lack of care. He'll bring her flowers or chocolates later, but his career will always take the literal helm in their lives, so no, her feelings aren't hurt.

She's just disappointed.

In less than five minutes, she's sliding into the back of a sleek BCM craft; BCM means Batrachomorpha. She forgets what the actual translation is, but it refers to vehicles that can be driven on land and in water, kind of like the sea runners Derivan technomancers use, but they don't change shape. Something like frog form, maybe? She gives the driver the address, then turns her attention to her holoscreen. She downloaded a new book just this morning and hasn't had the chance to read it yet.

It's as the main character is traveling by train to her doom alongside a drugged-up mentor and a chauvinistic sponsor that Magdalena looks up from her reading to check the time on her holo. They've been driving for over thirty minutes. Magdalena's home is only twenty minutes from the pier where the Vulcan's yacht was docked.

She looks out the window to check if maybe a traffic jam is what is slowing them down but finds instead that they are in a completely different part of the city.

"Umm, sir. I think you've taken a wrong turn somewhere. My house is in the suburbs."

The driver doesn't answer. He just keeps his focus forward, lights flashing across his face through the window. Now that she takes the time to look at him, she realizes just how young he is. Probably barely old enough to even work for transit services.

"Sir, you really need to turn around. My husband will be expecting me at home."

"Your husband isn't expecting you at home."

"Excuse me."

"Your husband is drinking champagne with the other fishmongers and their would-be king. He don't give a lick about you right now."

Magdalena's eyes meet the man's in the rearview mirror, and as she watches, he blinks, not with his eyelids but with a membrane that pulls horizontally across his eyes like window curtains.

"Stop the car right now."

A hand closes down on her wrist as she reaches for her comm unit. Someone is hiding in the seat behind her.

Magdalena nearly screams, but the sound dies as quickly as it arose when a knife pricks her throat.

"Take it easy, love. We're almost to our destination. Be still. Don't cause any trouble, and we won't hurt you."

Something about the voice of the person behind her puts her in a strange trance-like state. In her head, she knows that she should be screaming and fighting and throwing herself out of the goddamn car, but her body loses any and all interest in such things. It's like her fight or flight response has been turned off, the adrenaline sapped from her in the silky timbre of the voice in her ear. The person takes her comm from the seat, and the driver pulls into the driveway of an abandoned warehouse.

"We're here."

"Where is here?" she asks dully. She feels like she is floating, like the last time she went to the dentist. They gave her ketamine to keep her calm, and she'd been high as a kite for hours after the minor procedure.

"Just a dream, darling. You'll wake up any moment now."

The driver opens her door and guides her out of the car. He has his hands under her arms, and he keeps her steadily at his side as he walks her into the warehouse. It's a fishery, and the smell of salt and rotting ocean is enough to clear some of the endorphins running rampant through her system. The two men aren't really men at all. They're teenagers, and their features are similar enough that they could be brothers. One of them looks barely any older than her students while the other is barely entering puberty; both of them have vibrant copper hair and healthy beach tans like they frequent the water more than the land. But there is something unearthly about them. Something inhuman.

She starts to struggle at the sight of a metal chair, affixed with leather bindings. "Let go of me. I want to go home."

"Easy, easy," the voice from the car is back. "We just have a few questions for you. You don't want to ruin your pretty dress, do you?"

His grip on her tightens, and lucidity returns with the pain of the pressure.

"Fuck the dress and fuck you!"

She throws her head back, slamming the one holding her in the nose. He rears back, and she makes a break for it. Well, she tries to, anyway. She takes two steps toward the exit, and a sharp snap cracks through her as one of the cursed heels her husband bought her breaks. She tumbles forward, her ankle twisting on the wet floor, and just as she is about to hit the floor, the second teen catches her, lifting her like a sack of potatoes over one shoulder.

She kicks and pounds on his back with her fists, but either the youth is built like a tiger shark, or he has augmentations under the skin that make her tiny fists ineffectual. He sets her down in the chair. She makes to stand, wrestling her way out of the teen's hold, but the second she tries to put her weight on her foot, sharp shooting pain rips up her leg, and she falls back into the chair.

"What do you want? Money! Ha! Take what you want. The credit chip to my bank account is in my purse. Get yourself whatever toys kids your age are playing with."

"Alright, where's our mother?"

"Your what?"

"Our mother. Your bastard of a husband took her. We know. One of his ships got her."

"One of his ships. What the hell are you talking about?"

"Where is he keeping her?"

"My husband doesn't have your mother. My husband is an honest fisherman. What would he want with your mother?"

"Right—because honest fishermen don't dabble in illegal trade?"

"Illegal trade? I don't know what you're talking about."

"She's lying. She knows. How could she not know her husband is a tearer?"

A tearer? As in tearing up from crying? What's a tearer?

"Gustav, calm down. We won't gain anything from getting angry."

"Calm down! Mom has been missing for days, and you're telling me to calm down."

"Getting angry at a woman who doesn't know anything will not give us the answers we need, brother."

"Get real, Lee. I say we carve a message into her face and deliver her back home for her husband to read."

The older teenager, Lee, looks to his younger brother and begins to speak in a language Magdalena has never heard before. Not in a movie or TV show or even on the news. It's a flowy but guttural sounding tongue full of long unhurried vowels and high-pitched consonants. It reminds her of whale song, strangely enough.

As steady as the language sounds, the two boys are agitated. Both of their brows furrow and the lines of their shoulders tense as whatever conversation they are having unfolds.

While they fight amongst themselves, Magdalena kicks her shoes off her feet as quietly as she can. In the heel of her left foot is an emergency beacon. Once activated, it will call the local adept task force, the tracker functioning to lead them straight to her location. Magdalena never liked the idea of having something embedding into her body that could be used to trace her location or track her movements, but Adriano had been adamant she have one installed after the first wave of money found them. In case anything should ever happen. Anything like this.

With the big toe of her right foot, she feels for the tiny chip of metal that sits under the skin on the inside of her heel just below her ankle bone, and when she feels it, she digs harshly into her foot. The tiniest of clicks ricochets up her ankle, and she turns her attention back to the teens still arguing in front of her.

Gustav, the angrier of the two, gesticulates wildly toward Magdalena, the pitch of his voice rising from the dark timber of whale song to something closer to a dolphin's range. The knife in his hand slashes dangerously close to her arm. When the older tries to swipe the blade from the younger's hand, the younger shoves the elder away, turning to Magdalena, knife brandished towards her throat.

Magdalena closes her eyes.

"Stop!"

The knife never meets Magdalena's face.

Brown eyes open to find a translucent wall of light surrounding her. It glows a glossy pink sprinkled through with gold flecks. Vibrant and radiating warm soothing energy, the wall of light is even more stunning for the fact that it is presently holding the boy's knife back from stabbing Magdalena.

A magical shield?

"We agreed that we would do this better than them, remember?"

Out of the shadows steps the woman who has been haunting Magdalena's dreams. The Olga before her, dressed in a loose cotton dress and leather bodice, war-like markings painted across her face, looks nothing like the woman she encountered in the bar two nights ago. That woman had looked dressed for a party, clothed in a form-fitting dress, hair sexily tousled. This woman looks like a heathen from the hexen forests of the greater continent—a wanderer and a person apart. One of the people the League warns against.

Suddenly, the simple double circle tattoo on Olga's shoulder doesn't seem like a tattoo at all.

"What's the point of having a higher moral code if it doesn't save the people you care about?"

"This woman has nothing to do with your mother's disappearance."

"Her husband is the one that took her."

"We do not know that for sure."

"Ares saw his ship. It can't be anyone else."

"We do not know for sure, and until we do know for certain, you will not be maiming anyone."

"What would a witch know?"

Witch? Olga's a witch. Well, that probably makes a lot of sense now that Magdalena thinks about it. She is, after all, presently sitting inside of a bubble made by the woman herself, a bubble that is currently shielding her from whatever bloodthirsty creatures these two boys must be.

"This witch is the reason you are still alive, boy," says Olga. "You thought you could threaten the Goblin King into looking for your mother? You're lucky he didn't remove your head from your body outright."

"And we're supposed to be grateful that a no-account witch with no offensive powers was allowed to help us?"

"If you think going on the offensive in a city of this size will save your mother, you're not just wrong, kid. You're dead wrong."

Gustav opens his mouth to protest again, but Lee interrupts. "Gustav, stop. Olga is right. This is not the way."

"Why should we care what a witch has to say, Lee? We aren't beholden to them just because some thousand-years dead witch made our existence possible."

"And she has chosen to help us out of the goodness of her heart. The spell-folk need to stick together if we ever want to live in peace."

The boy crosses his arms across his chest, glaring at Lee. "I don't see anyone hunting her kind for greed."

"You're right," inserts Olga. "The League doesn't hunt my kind for monetary gain. They hunt my kind for sport."

That seems to cow the younger.

Lee steps forward and takes the knife from his brother's hand

"We would not even have come this far without Olga's help. That you would speak to her in such a way is disgraceful."

"But—"

"We will find her, okay? We'll find her, and everything is going to be just fine."

"But what if we're too late? You know what they do to them when they've gotten everything they can."

"Don't think that way—"

BOOM!

The deafening boom of a sonic wave goes off outside the building, making her ears ring. Shards of shattering glass rain down from the warehouse wall. Olga's protective bubble keeps her face and neck from harm, needle-sharp splinters scattering away as they hit the wall of pink magic.

"Adepts!"

The witch erects another shield as aether pistols open fire on her kidnappers.

"Lee!"

The older boy begins to sing. Or at least the closer word Magdalena can think of to describe what Lee does is singing. He's not exactly opening his mouth or humming, and yet an aura expands from his essence. Vibrations extend from his aura in visible arcs of energy in the deepest shade of blue. They resonant like tuning forks throughout the room, so potent, Magdalena can feel them reverberating through her bones. The sonorous tendrils of wild sound reach out all the way to the windows and beyond, and the open fire on the room ceases.

Is this what siren-song sounds like?

"Get to the docks!" commands Olga. "Don't look back. I'll take care of her. If there are adepts here, a technomancer is sure to follow."

Without argument, the teens do as they are told, running for the far exit that will lead them to the swirling ocean outside. Meanwhile, Olga makes her way to Magdalena. When she goes to untie the bindings at her wrists and ankles, Magdalena jerks back. "Don't touch me!"

"I'm going to untie you."

"I'm not going anywhere with you."

"I'm not going to hurt you."

"I don't believe you."

Olga recoils from Magdalena, as though she isn't the greater threat between the two of them and Magdalena is in any way capable of hurting her.

"These boys kidnapped you because they're desperate. They want their mother back, and if they don't find her quickly enough, they'll never see her alive again."

"And like I told them, I haven't a clue where their mother is or whatever she is. Leave me and my husband alone. We have nothing to do with her disappearing."

Olga just looks sadly at Magdalena.

"That's a lovely necklace. Did your husband give it to you?"

Her necklace? The single pearl drop necklace around her neck. Adriano had it made especially for her.

"It was an anniversary gift."

Olga just nods.

"You best make sure you don't lose it. It's all that remains of the person who made it."

Magdalena frowns. What on earth does that even mean? But before she can voice her question, raised voices shout through the warehouse doors. The adepts are pounding on the metal to get it to open, and it won't be long until it gives even with Olga's magical forcefield keeping them at bay.

"You should go," says Magdalena, surprising herself. "Unless you want to get killed."

Olga laughs, and it is exactly the same way she laughed when Magdalena drank too much of her drink too quickly. The blonde reaches forward and touches Magdalena on the forehead.

"Be well, *Skönhet*."

Olga's fingers are cool on her overheated brow, and the wash of magic that spills over her is warm and familiar, reminiscent of the woman's touch during intimacy, and suddenly, Magdalena feels like she's been filled to the brim with want, the void of the last few days now overflowing with the wash of Olga's magic. Magic she should be afraid of. Witchcraft—blasphemous, heathenous, dangerous witchcraft, used to invite pestilence, misfortune, and destruction on humans like Olga. Yet, Olga's magic had protected her from the blade of a knife and the bite of broken glass.

Magdalena's eyes slide shut as relief, unbidden and unexpected, drains the tension from her body. *Is this what it feels like to be bewitched?*

Olga's touch disappears from her forehead as the warehouse doors burst open. There is shouting and flashing lights and the sound of water splashing. Someone is talking to her, but they sound far off and distant, like they are on the other side of a glass wall.

"Sra. Villanueva, have they hurt you in any way?"

All she can do is shake her head as the world pixelates, and her eyes roll into the back of her head. The last of her adrenaline sapped from her body, the imminent crash shuts down her system before she can go into shock.

5

Drum and Bass

O LGA'S KISSES TASTE LIKE LICORICE AND *sugar. Her skin is smooth, unmarred by augmentations, and so pale it seems to glitter in the moonlight. She unwraps Magdalena like a present with gentle but excited hands. Under her back, the sand is still warm from the day...*

Magdalena wakes up to Adriano's fluffy, pinched eyebrows. "Magda! You're awake. Nurse!"

He hasn't shaved. His scruff makes him look less like one of the attractive bad boys on television and more like the sorry sods who watch too much porn and sniff their underwear to check if they're clean or not.

She blinks twice and pushes the bitter thoughts from her mind.

He's still wearing his tux. *What time is it? Did he come straight from the Vulcan's yacht?* Did she interrupt his networking opportunity or was he already on the way home?

"Magda, how are you feeling, mi amor?"

She opens her mouth to speak, but dust may as well have puffed from her mouth for how dry and cottony her tongue and gums feel.

"W-Waaahhhateer," she rasps out.

Adriano seems to get the message, offering her a cup from the bedside table. He guides the straw into her mouth, and she drinks deep until the cobwebs have washed down her throat.

"What time is it?"

"Almost five in the morning."

What time did she leave the party? It was early. Maybe 9:30?

"What happened to the...the—"

"Don't you worry, dear. They won't hurt you again. The adepts got there before those monsters could hurt you, and they're already on full alert looking for the hexen who escaped. Fabien wants to ask you some questions. Do you think you're up for it?"

The hexen who escaped? Olga?

Magdalena nods.

"I'll call him while the doctor checks on you. I'm sure he'll be here quickly. They've been searching for the witch all night."

Witch... The witch got away. Thank—

She cuts off the thought before she can even finish thinking it. Olga is a witch. A witch! She probably cast some sort of spell on Magdalena the other night. That's why she hasn't been able to get her out of her head. That's why she's been dreaming about her. That's why she'd been unfaithful to her husband in the first place. All because of a witch's spell.

That must be it!

At least, Magdalena convinces herself that that has to be it.

Adriano leaves her side, already pulling his comm unit from his pocket, and the doctor comes in. The woman asks her the usual questions. What's her name? What year is it? How old is she? What's her occupation? And as far as Magdalena can tell, she scores full marks on the examination.

"Alright. I've checked you over for magic sickness, and it looks like you got lucky as far as magical exposure goes because there's nothing in your system."

Magdalena blinks. "Nothing?"

The doctor smiles, a full smile that reaches all the way to his eyes and makes his dimples sparkle on the sides of his face.

"Mhmm. You're completely clean. Either you escaped unscathed, or your filtration system managed to get it all out. You should thank your husband for that. I know those new tech designs are experimental, but they seem to be doing their job. He told me he's the one who insisted you have the augmentation done."

Magdalena frowns. That's not right. Even since the surgery, she's never had a 0% reading of magical radiation in her system. Too much exposure as a child.

"But I've had Wúxíng Syndrome since I was seven."

The doctor looks at her skeptically. "There's no evidence of that from your scans."

"My grandmother died from it, and not long after, they realized I had it too. We used to live out in the country..."

"Well, perhaps you were misdiagnosed. You have no evidence of magical radiation anywhere in your system despite the close contact with Hexen."

That's because magic sickness isn't spread by Hexen. It's like radiation. People are exposed to it just by living in Deus, and the only way to filter it out is through routine maintenance and/or magical exercise. That's why Magdalena has a filtration system in her augmentations, not that it does much to keep her from getting sick from time to time anyway.

"Your augmentations kept you from going into shock, so you should be good to go. There'll be a bit of bruising around your wrists, and we've treated your ankle with a stim. You should be able to return to work by tomorrow, but take your time. You've just been through a very traumatic experience. If you need an extra day from work, just let us know, and we'll take care of the excuse to the academy."

"Th-thank you, doctor."

"I'll have my intern bring up your discharge papers."

The doctor leaves and in her wake, the techno-mancer enters.

While she's never met the man herself, Fabien is well known among the people of Acapōlco. Born and raised in this very city, he was the last person to achieve the title tech-nomancer from Acapōlco—to their city's pride. Originally a fisherman's son, he trained himself into peak physical condi-tion, and at eighteen, he booked himself a ticket to the capital for the Derivan hosted technomancer trials and came out on the other side a titan among men. It was said that he even tutored Tlanextli himself when the Vulcan was growing up and preparing for his trials.

But that was years ago. About ten years back, Fabien all but retired from active duty and returned home to live the quiet life with his partner. Now the man just looks tired and drawn. The bags under his eyes are heavy from having worked Magdalena's case all night, and even his weapon, a brass plated harpoon gun, seems dull in comparison to when Magdalena saw him at the party. He'd been all bright and shiny then with his pressed tux and sparkling smile.

Magdalena almost asks him how he's holding up because clearly he has been through a tougher night than she. She was just kidnapped. Nothing stressful about that, really. But at least she slept through the brute of gloomtide.

"Sra. Villanueva, I presume."

"Yes, sir," she answers, hands folded in her lap.

"Fabien De La Rose," he introduces himself, and she shakes his offered hand. She's not sure why, but she expected it to be coarser, more weathered like a sailor's, but his hands are smooth save for the line of a tech augmentation graphed below his skin. *Maybe that's why his hands are in such good con-dition?* His augmentations. They do say that technomancer grade enhancements are of the highest quality. "I wanted to see how you were holding up. I understand that the last few hours have been trying for you, but if you are up for it. I have a couple of questions for you."

Magdalena adjusts the blanket over her lap. "Of-of course."

"Wonderful, if you'll give me a moment." Fabien opens up a panel in his right forearm to reveal a circular disk, the dermis laid over the augmentation folding back like a sleeve. It's an outdated augmentation, one that is cringeworthy to look at now, but technomancers are so heavily technolyzed that replacement augmentations and upgrades simply cannot be performed after they reach a certain age, and Fabien is way past his prime, sitting at around 75 years old.

He activates the revealed device, and a little red light turns on at its center. A beam of line extends out from its core and scans the room from ceiling to floor with Magdalena and Fabien in between.

"Here we are. Just a holo-recording that I can reference back to later. This will act as an official record of our conversations if your case makes it to trial."

"If?"

"Yes, Sra. If it goes to trial, meaning in the event mundane humans or other human+ were responsible for your kidnapping, but chances are these were hexen of some kind if the testimonies of the adepts first to arrive at the scene are any indication."

"The hexen won't be tried."

"They've proven themselves to be violent, so no. Of course not. They aren't human, anyway, so they don't have a right to a trial."

Something about that statement doesn't sit well in Magdalena's stomach. *They aren't human.* Then, what are they? Animals? None of them looked like animals. Not even the young man who was so frightened by the prospect of losing his mother that he threatened to carve up Magdalena's face. Was he to be put down like a mad cow? Deemed unfit and dangerous, and therefore forfeiting his right to life?

"Please, state your name, age, and occupation for the record."

Magdalena clears the cotton from her throat.

"My name is Magdalena Villanueva. I am 28 years old, and I am an old-world literature teacher at the academy."

"And what event occurred last night that you activated your emergency beacon?"

"I was... I was kidnapped by two teenagers. They, um, they took me to a fishing warehouse by the docks and asked me questions."

"What questions were these?"

"They wanted to know where their mother was. They kept saying my husband took her, and I don't understand why they kept saying that."

"And what is your husband's name and occupation?"

"Adriano Villanueva. He's a mining fleet owner. We were at the Vulcan's Seafarer's Ball."

"And why wasn't your husband with you at the time of your kidnapping?"

"Oh, I left early because I felt ill. So, I called a Ryde. That's how they kidnapped me. One of them was the driver."

"We found the vehicle at the scene. There are some fingerprints, and one of them left a backpack inside full of spare clothes. Was there anything to remember about them that seemed strange?"

"They spoke in this weird language that I've never heard before. It sounded like they were singing but they weren't. I don't know what it was."

"Did either of them use magic?"

"No. At least, I don't think they did. Though one of them started making strange sounds once the adept force arrived."

"What kind of sounds?"

"It was like singing, but he wasn't moving his mouth. It wasn't humming either. It was like when someone tries to talk underwater."

"Were these the only two you remember? You're certain?"

Magdalena hesitates and then:

"I don't remember anyone else," she lies, without properly understanding why. She only knows that she doesn't want him to know about Olga.

Fabien makes a noncommittal humming sound and adjusts a setting on his recording device.

"Thank you, Sra. All I can say now is that we are tracking your kidnappers with as many resources as we can expend. We have good visual recordings of them, but the two disappeared into the water just as high tide was rolling in."

"Hide tide!"

Were they mad? Only someone with swimming modifications and a few years of experience could maneuver the stronger currents that throttle through the beaches like clockwork. There was a reason Acapõlco had restrictions on swimming hours for the bay. Between the currents and the rocky coral reefs below the surface, it was easy to drown or bludgeon yourself to death during high tide.

Fabien nods.

"And we never saw them come back up again. It's likely they drowned trying to get away. So, unless there was someone else there, I don't think you have anything to worry about, Sra. Villanueva."

Magdalena blinks. "I see. Thank you, Sr. De La Rose."

"Not at all, Sra. Thank you for your time. I'll leave you be. I'm sure your husband is anxious to get you home, safe and sound."

Adriano takes her home. He fusses and dotes on her even though she keeps telling him she is fine. Her ankle is just a little sore, and okay, she still thinks she's been bewitched, but she isn't about to tell Adriano that as he tucks her into bed.

It is only after he takes a call on his comm that he decides to leave her be. It helps that apparently the call was urgent, and his presence is needed at the docks. Could it be related to her kidnapping? No. Fabien said the two boys were probably dead in the water, but Olga? What if Olga is still after them? Did Magdalena make a mistake by keeping silent about the woman? No, not the woman. *La Bruja*.

As soon as the front door closes behind Adriano, Magdalena is up and searching the web for remedies for bewitchment and love spells. What she draws up is a strange mishmash of methods and ingredients that seem as arbitrary as anything. Tuck a goose egg under your pillow and in the morning crack it over the head of a donkey? Yeah, like everyone just had a goose and a donkey around to do that kind of thing with.

Eventually, she finds a recipe for a drink she can make that should "counter" a love spell and heads to the store to scavenge the ingredients.

As she's walking the aisles, heading for the dairy section, she feels like everyone is looking at her. It's kind of like the way she felt at the party last night, only worse. She has oranges, cinnamon sticks, black licorice, and black candles in her basket, and she feels like everyone around knows something about her she doesn't and it's unnerving. No one here even knows her name. Adriano always tells her that she likes to overthink things.

It is as she is sticking her head into the fridge that someone actually approaches her.

"If you're looking for something to ward away love, you should add soy milk to the mix. Oh, and add garlic and onion to whatever you're planning to blend. The more the better. That way no one wants to kiss you."

Magdalena jolts up, hitting her head on the shelf above where she had stuck her head in the fridge.

It's Olga. The woman is dressed in simple jeans and a t-shirt. There is nothing of the savage Magdalena remembers from last night.

"What are you doing here? Are you following me?"

The blonde looks from side to side then to the basket in her hand. It's full of packaged fish and vegetables.

"Grocery shopping. You think those boys live on air?"

Those boys? The teenagers. The ones Fabien said should be somewhere at the bottom of a coral reef.

"You're a witch! I should be sounding the alarms right now."

"But you won't."

"And why is that?"

"Because I protected you. Those Tidewalkers are young and scared. It's natural for them to react with violence. That's why I went with them to make sure they didn't hurt anyone."

Tidewalkers? What the hell is a tidewalker?

"I don't know what you're talking about. Leave me alone before I call for security."

Magdalena turns to leave, violently thrusting her basket between herself and Olga. She hears a cracking sound as several cinnamon sticks protest the harsh jolt. ¡Pinche m*ierda!*

"Wait, please!" calls Olga.

Despite everything that she knows and believes, she stops, her bag of groceries dangling limp from her forearm.

"I know you're still shaken about what happened, and I'm sorry about the boys. They shouldn't have done what they did, but let me explain. The boys are worried about their mother, and you might be the only person who can help us find her."

"You want to talk to me, a transhuman, in the middle of a grocery store, about—" the teller looks over, and Magdalena flinches, lowering her voice and leaning closer to the witch, "—about hexen problems."

The witch winces at that, probably realizing her error.

"How about a coffee? I know a place nearby. My treat. Oh, and coffee beans are an instant remedy for love spells by the way, so it'll serve two purposes."

Without receiving Magdalena's affirmative, the woman turns and walks to the teller to pay for her groceries.

Magdalena blinks, feeling more than a little stunned in the other woman's wake, and then, feeling more than a little like she is walking into a trap, she follows, and if she grabs a few cloves of garlic on her way to the checkout line, it isn't because she believes anything Olga has to say.

6

Tea for Two

MAGDALENA GOES WITH OLGA TO A nearby cafe. There aren't many other patrons, and they are able to seat themselves at a table far enough away from anyone that they can converse in relative privacy. It's quiet and intimate and entirely inappropriate for her to be there with the woman she not only cheated on her husband with but also the woman who was involved in her kidnapping just hours ago.

A young waiter appears at her elbow as she is setting her canvas grocery bag on the floor.

"What can I get for you, ladies?"

"Un café latte, por favor."

"She'll have it decaf," inserts Olga.

Magda furrows her brow, indignant. The waiter's eyes slide back and forth between the two of them.

"Are you ordering for me as well?" snips Magdalena.

The woman looks surprised for a moment.

"Oh, you don't—I mean, not at all, but trust me. You want decaf. The caffeinated here makes my head buzz, and it's pretty late in the afternoon anyway. You don't want to mess up your sleep cycle."

"Hmph. *Bueno bien. Entonces* decaf it is."

The pen scratches happily over the notepad. "*Si, senora.* And you, ma'am?"

"I'll have an egg coffee."

Magda glares at the witch across from her.

"Decaf as well," she adds, sheepishly.

"*Perfecto.* I'll have those out to you right away."

The youth pivots toward the bar to put in their orders, and Magdalena crosses her arms in front of her chest, glaring at Olga with indignation.

"I take it you have questions."

"You'd better believe I have questions."

"Then ask them, Magdalena."

The way Magdalena's name rolls off Olga's tongue makes it sound like a rich coconut and chocolate sorbet, each syllable carefully folded over the tongue and passed through her lips with a chaste kiss. A shiver shoots down her spine, and her core tightens.

It stuns her for just long enough that she forgets they are in a public place, and her charisma enhancers whirr to life in response, releasing persuasive enzymes into the air to make someone more amiable to her. Normally, she would only use them in her classroom to make sure her students are paying attention, but because of her body's response to Olga, her system has rewired the usual settings to exude the more primal hormones that the body generates to encourage sexual attraction.

"You don't need to use pheromones on me, Lena. I don't mind answering your questions. Besides, I like you well enough without."

Magdalena blushes and scolds herself. ¡Agarre, Lena! ¡No seas estúpida!

"So, what's a tidewalker?"

Olga leans back in her seat with a crooked grin on her face. There is sadness in the corners of her lips.

"You've heard of mermaids, I assume."

"Yes. They're monsters that drown sailors at sea."

"That does happen sometimes, but what they don't tell you is that the men seduced by their siren songs are rapists and thieves. Men who lie and cheat and do more harm than good. Their own lust is what lures them to the depths and they drown in their own avarice."

"No. That isn't true. Mermaids feed on innocents."

"If that's what you believe, believe it. I'm not here to change a mind that doesn't want to be changed. Ignorance is a willful infection, after all."

Anger flares up. Magda isn't ignorant! She received some of the best education in Deriva. She has a degree in psychology and literature. And this witch who has probably never even seen the inside of a university campus is accusing her of being ignorant. Preposterous! But... Why did her words sting so?

Magda is about to spit as much when their coffee arrives. She bites her tongue and nods thankfully at the waiter. When he leaves them with napkins, she attempts to bring the conversation back on track.

"What do mermaids have to do with anything anyway? They never come close enough to the shore to warrant technomancer attention."

"Tidewalkers are the children that result from the unions between sailors and mermaids."

"Unions between sailors and mermaids? You mean when humans are dragged out to sea by siren-song and drowned?"

The witch nods. "Sometimes the encounters result in children."

"How is that possible?" They're completely different species!

"Witch magic. A long time ago, merfolk were dying out due to infertility. They aren't monsters but they are very much like their fish companions, cold-blooded and loveless. They invoked the help of witches to regain their ability to procreate. The population recovered, but it had unexpected side-effects. Mermaids were now able to become pregnant by human males."

Gemini Twins! Really?!

"So ... Tidewalkers."

"Yes. Hexen that are half mermaid, half human. They only exist as the byproduct of age-old witchcraft much like lycans and vampires. It is why they're considered hexen rather than fae."

"How come I've never heard of them?"

Olga shrugs.

"There aren't very many of them, and ironically enough, the fertility magic that makes them possible does not get passed down. They are born sterile. Most mermaids spurn their half-human spawn. They can't live their whole lives in the water, so they end up raised by sea witches or unknowing humans, but the mermaid we are looking for is quite unique. She kept in touch with her babies as they grew."

"So, when those two boys were asking me where their mother was..."

"They were asking what your husband had done with his most recent mermaid catch."

What!

"My husband doesn't fish for mermaids. He doesn't even fish! He's a miner, for crying out loud."

"Are you sure about that?"

"Of course, I'm sure! He's an honest seaman who built himself up from nothing."

"Yes, and I'm sure there are plenty of good men that have worked for their good fortunes, but your husband went from nothing to owning a deep-sea mining company almost overnight."

"Are you accusing my husband of pearling mermaids?"

"Where do you think the pearl on your necklace came from?"

Magda's hand flies to her throat and the teardrop pearl dangling there. She'd always loved the color; turquoise is her favorite shade of blue and the speckles of yellow and green make the stone glitter in the right lighting. *A unique find,* her husband had said when he gifted it to her on their third wedding anniversary.

"No, that... That can't be true."

Olga sighs, looking away from Magdalena to stare down into her coffee, sadly. "Give me your hand."

"What for?"

"You can trust me. I promise I won't hurt you, not purposely anyway. Sometimes, the truth is more hurtful than the lie."

Magda swallows, suddenly afraid. Not of the witch in front of her. No. She is afraid of her words. And isn't that the root of it? Fear of the unknown. Magdalena has never had to be brave. She isn't an adept or a technomancer. She never had an interest in such a lifestyle. All she ever wanted was a family and a lecture room where she could share classical literature with students thirsty for knowledge, and she's damn good at it, too. The Vulcan of Deriva didn't ask her to tutor his children for no reason.

Yet here she is, sitting across from a witch with two options in front of her: bravery or cowardice, and she doesn't know which one is more dangerous.

But Olga's eyes are so open and vibrant. An otherworldly purple flecked with turquoise, and even though their colors are nothing alike, they remind her terribly of Freya Nocturne, the alluring woman who had comforted her on a ship and told her she hoped one day for her little girl to be as learned and wise as Magdalena. She wanted to trust those eyes, and she doesn't know if the compulsion comes from her own gut or some quiet magic woven into her perception. Maybe it doesn't matter.

So, she slides her hand across the table.

Olga's hands may be rough from whatever labors she's toiled through, but they are warm and unbelievably gentle as they guide Magdalena's hand palm up. Olga studies Magda's hand the way Magda studies manuscripts, her eyes coaxing secrets from the lines before her. She traces a finger across the center of her palm. Pleasure tickles across her skin and goosebumps crop up along her arm.

"Do you see this line here?" The witch traces the line that curls towards her wrist, and Magdalena nods. "This is your life line. It isn't very long, but it's prominent. You'll live a rich life with many experiences, perhaps even adventures. And though your death will be unexpected, it will come without regrets."

"Unexpected?"

Olga nods. "I can't tell you what it might be. You may fall asleep and never wake up. It might be an accident. But your family will be by your side when it happens."

"Will they—"

"I can't answer anything about them. This is your palm, not theirs." She moves on to the next two lines. "Your fate and heart lines are intertwined which usually means that you will fall in love with your soulmate."

"Soulmates are for hexen tales."

"If you say so," says Olga, non-arguably. "But you've met them very recently. Only in the last day or so."

"That's not possible. My husband and I have been married for over three years and together for even longer."

Those icy blue eyes slide to Magdalena's face, slow as a drifting glacier. The look is not unlike those first few glances in the darkness of Le Pier Revue. They say intimacy and sultry gazes are far more potent between sheets of shadows, yet in the afternoon light streaming in through the window of a quaint coffee shop, where there are no shadows, no colored lighting, or the swirling curls of cigarette smoke to hide behind, that look seems all the more penetrating. Magdalena feels even more bare before this woman than when she was lying naked beside her on a beach towel while a star-studded ocean lapped at their feet.

When Olga speaks, her words shatter fragile walls of the glass house Magdalena has been living in her whole life.

"Your soulmate isn't a man, Lena."

And the heat that builds in Magdalena's core is so jarring, she pulls her hand out of the witch's grasp and bolts for the door.

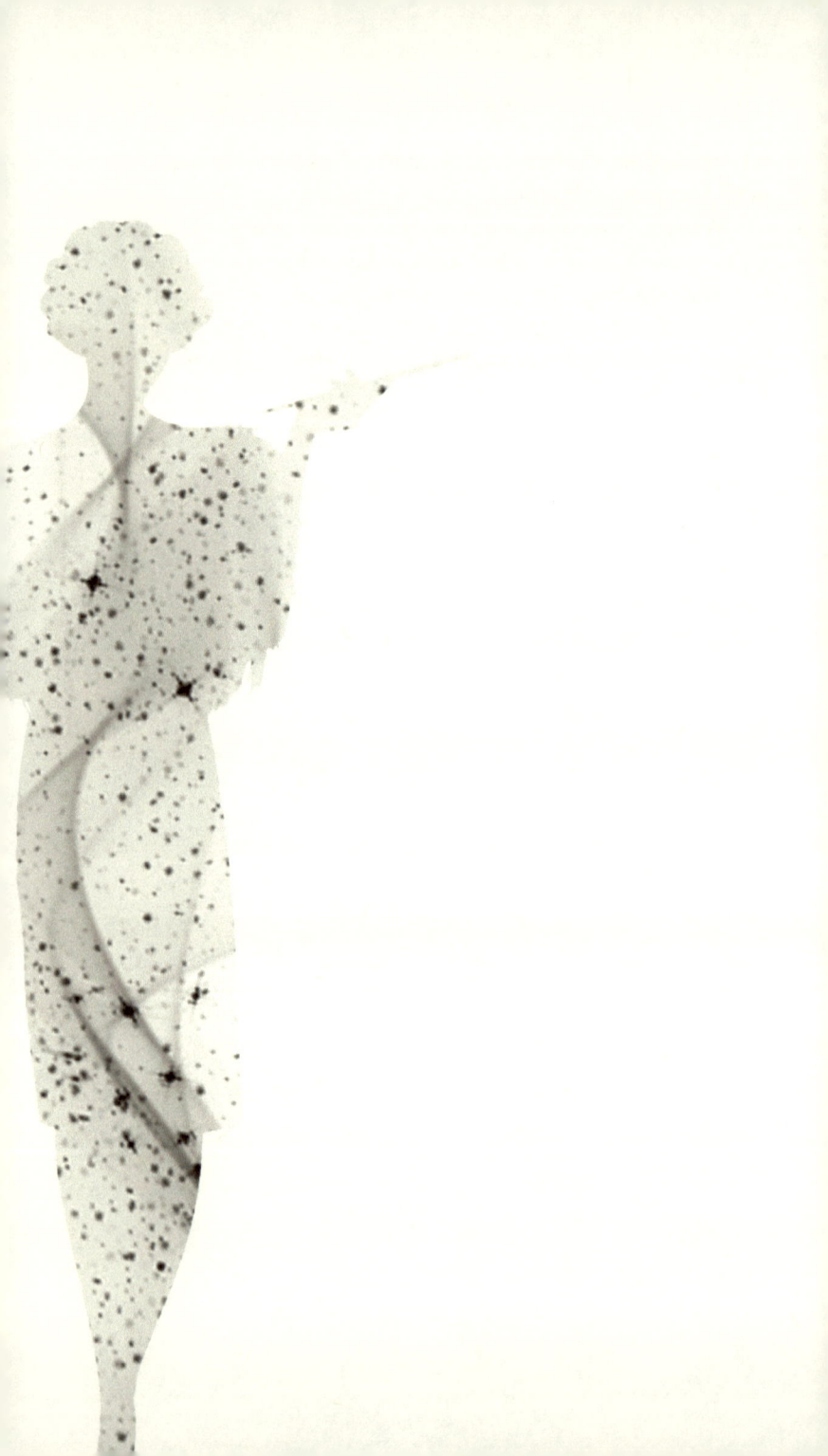

7

Vibrato

O LGA'S LIPS TRAIL BETWEEN THE VALLEY
of Magdalena's breasts, her chest heaving with exertion
as she comes down from the first orgasm she's ever had without the
help of a vibrator. The other woman's lips meet hers.

Goddess above, she can taste herself on the woman's tongue.

"That's a beautiful necklace." Pale fingers glide across the glittering pearl at her throat. "Who gave it to you?"

Magdalena touches the pearl around her neck. "My husband—"

She cuts herself off with a gasp, and for a moment, Olga's eyes
reflect like a cat's in the dark, but then Magdalena blinks, and the
reflection of light is gone. Must have been a passing boat light.

"Your husband?"

Magdalena swallows the bile down before it can spill out of
her big, fat mouth.

"My husband gave it to me for our anniversary."

Olga hums.

"He has good taste."

Mouth dry, Magdalena sits up; Olga moves off of her shoulder,
giving her space to move. She turns her back on the woman,
already reaching for her clothing.

"Where are you going?"

She stops at the touch of a hand on her elbow.

"Away." No. "Home," she corrects herself. "I should get home."

"Why? I thought we were enjoying each other's company."

"You must think me horrible."

Olga tilts her head, shrugging her shoulders. "No."

"No?" Magdalena turns around, wide-eyed with disbelief. "I just cheated on my husband with you. How could you not think I'm an awful person?!"

Olga rises from her place in the sand, scooting closer to Magdalena. She tucks a stray strand of dark hair behind Magdalena's ear before pressing a chaste kiss to her cheek.

"If you think you should go, then go, but I don't think you're horrible, Magda." A kiss to her other cheek. "I just think you're human."

And the kiss to her lips washes away any and all desire to run away from the woman before her.

Magdalena runs from Olga, runs from a woman who has, in such a short amount of time, laid her bare and stripped her to her roots. Olga's words haunt her in more ways than one. Her soulmate isn't a man? How dare she say something like that to her! Magdalena has never been attracted to women, at least not the way she is attracted to Olga. And soulmates aren't real, anyway. They're just hexen stories made up to make everyone believe that they are made of stardust and that they weren't all alone in the universe.

But they are alone, and Magdalena most assuredly feels terribly, terribly alone as she makes her way home.

She doesn't even stop to call a Ryde. She just walks her way home on her injured ankle, now throbbing with every step and practically shouting at her with each step. It isn't until she is through her front door and throwing the dead bolt that she realizes she forgot her groceries at the coffee shop.

She curses at the comedic ridiculousness of it. She didn't even get a sip of the coffee she ordered. Oh, well. She was never a fan of decaf anyway.

Now that she's home though, she doesn't know what to do with herself.

"Adriano?" she calls into the house, overly large for two people. The space is so empty her call practically echoes back to her. Of course, he isn't back yet. He'd left for work. It'll be hours still before he returns home. The foyer yawns before her, more intimidating than ever before, and she shuffles her way through the neck of the house to the kitchen.

Her medications from the hospital are on the counter still. She isn't due for another of the antihistamines, but the pharmacist told her she could take the painkillers as needed, and considering she just marched herself a few dozen blocks, her ankle is incredibly angry with her, definitely protesting the decision.

She takes a pill and downs a half glass of water with it. Leaning heavily against the island counter, her hand goes to the pearl pendant at her collar.

It can't be a mermaid tear. There's no way. Adriano wouldn't do that. Tearing. She's heard of the practice. It isn't illegal, per se. Merfolk aren't considered human after all, but the idea of tormenting something to tears just leaves a bad taste in Magdalena's mouth. Especially something as ethereal and powerful as a mermaid. Siren horror stories aside, Derivans learn early on to respect the rulers of the oceans. Mermaids are fearsome creatures with the power to control the ocean's rises and falls, and mermen are even more terrifying, able to call down tempests and sink ships if they feel their homes and families encroached upon.

There is a reason only technomancers go after them and fishing ships are cautioned not to drop their nets near known merfolk-occupied waters. But for the fishermen willing to risk it, riches untold are the promised reward if they could bag a mermaid and get it to cry. But to get a soulless creature to cry? The sadism necessary!

No. It can't be true. Adriano wouldn't do something so foolish, so cruel.

And yet, Magdalena finds herself pulled, as though by an unseen force to the thick island evergreen wood door that looms at the top of the hallway. She has passed this door every day since they first moved into this house, and she hasn't set foot into it since her husband claimed it as his office. The only room in her home that she has been restricted from, and she has been so complacent, she never thought to question why she wasn't allowed in a part of her own home. She opens the door now.

It isn't even locked.

The door swings open with hardly a sound to reveal a well-organized study. A large important-looking desk acts as the focal point of the room, guarded on both sides by filing cabinets and bookshelves. Adriano's old fishing trophies hang on plaques on the wall, the largest of which is a purple-finned marlin, its sword-like nose speckled with golden scales. She'd forgotten that her husband, despite his career as a marine miner, used to enjoy fishing for sport. How could she have forgotten such a thing?

She approaches the desk. It's neat and organized, the way one would expect the desk of an important businessman or CEO to keep his workspace tidy. There is a neat pile of freshly signed documents, shipment reports, and financing updates. To the left is the expensive fountain pen Magdalena had engraved for him for his last birthday. The holo-projection unit inlaid into the center of the desk is quiet for the moment, darkened in hibernation. Magdalena doesn't dare risk turning it on, though; it's connected directly to Adriano's optic interface.

She starts with the filing cabinets, opening each drawer and fingering through the contents. Then she goes into the files on the desk. Nothing there other than what she expected to find. After about an hour of pillaging her husband's study, she finds nothing even remotely suspicious and breathes a sigh of relief for it.

See? Magdalena was right. Her husband would never do anything like tear a mermaid.

It's as she is tucking everything back into place that she finds the lock. It doesn't look like a lock at first, just an edged hole at the back center of the drawer, but when she checks with her nails, she finds the edge of a lid of some kind. A false bottom? Puzzled, she goes to the other cabinet to compare and finds nothing there.

She empties out the contents of the drawer. Trying to pry the panel out with her bare hands first is no use at all, and she doesn't want to scratch up the varnish by grabbing a tool, so she scouts the office for a key. She goes through the desk again. She scours the bookshelves. She checks under every piece of furniture in the room and nothing. *Does he keep the key on him?*

Where would Adriano hide a key he didn't want anyone else to find? A key that might conceal illicit fishing affairs. *Right!*

She moves a chair to the wall where the marlin arches against its plaque. Careful not to knock the fish off the wall, she traces her hands up and down the plastered scales and finds the key in the animal's mouth. It's small and pewter black and looks just the right size to fit in the little keyhole in the drawer. Under the panel is a single data chip.

With trembling fingers, Magdalena picks up the chip and carries it to the desk. She sits, gingerly arranging herself as comfortably as she can, and inserts the storage drive into her cellular. She waits, watching the percentage wheel as the drive installs itself, and when the navigation window opens, there is a singular folder labeled: Fishing. She clicks the file open.

What she finds horrifies her.

There are photographs, video recordings, bargaining contracts. Comparisons on different kinds of fishhooks and netting. A summary of financial worth, contracts with jewelers, and large sums of money being moved back and forth with the current total ending in the negative. Largely in the negative. A huge deficit of money was recently borrowed from Lucretia Boleria, the same woman who approached her at the Seafarer's Ball. There's a deed to a shipping container with an address that is too far away from the trade docks to be of any use as an actual transport unit.

Worst of all is the footage.

Tangled hair, flailing fishtails, blood the color of the ocean, and inhuman screams. Mermaids... being tortured to tears. Tortured to death.

Her heart drowns, a greater shock setting into her system than the shock of being kidnapped by a pair of teenagers. Of falling for a witch. Of being told her soulmate isn't a man. Magdalena's whole body shudders, her stomach dropping out of her belly, and the tears streak down her face in rivers. A hand slaps over her mouth to keep herself from screaming.

How could he do this? How could anybody do this?

Magdalena looks up as the sound of footsteps click up the hallway, and she hurries to shove everything back where it was but keeps the data chip, slamming the file cabinet drawer shut. Wiping her tears from her face, she shoves the data chip into her pocket and sits back at the chair. As a final measure to wave off suspicion, she yanks on the pearl necklace around her neck, breaking it from the chain. There, now Adriano will think she is upset about the necklace.

"Magda, what are you doing in here?"

"Oh, h-hi honey."

He sees her face, tear-stained and distraught and immediately becomes her white knight.

"Magda, sweetheart. What's wrong? Are you hurt?"

"It's nothing. I just. I was-I was looking for the jeweler information on where you commissioned my anniversary necklace. I realized today that when those beasts kidnapped me that they broke the clasp."

"Oh, darling. That's nothing to cry over. Here, why don't you give it to me? I can take care of it."

"I know, dear, but you've been so stressed, what with work and the vandalism. The last thing you need to be worrying about is a silly necklace."

"A necklace that was broken by a pair of ruffians who attacked my wife to get to me," he huffs, making his way toward her. "Darling, you've undergone a traumatic experience. What those monsters might have done to you ... I can't even imagine. I've been selfish. Here you are suffering, worrying about me, when I should be worrying about you. How about this? We'll go away for a couple of days. Take a vacation, just you and me, and who knows? Maybe the time away will be good for... ya know."

He looks down at her stomach, and it's anything but sexy the way he looks at her. The sting of the fertility treatments resonates through her, months of disappointments, moon cycles come and gone without progress. Sometimes she wonders if she's just another investment to him, one that he hasn't gotten to bear fruit.

Olga's never looked at her like that. Not even when she was more valuable dead than alive.

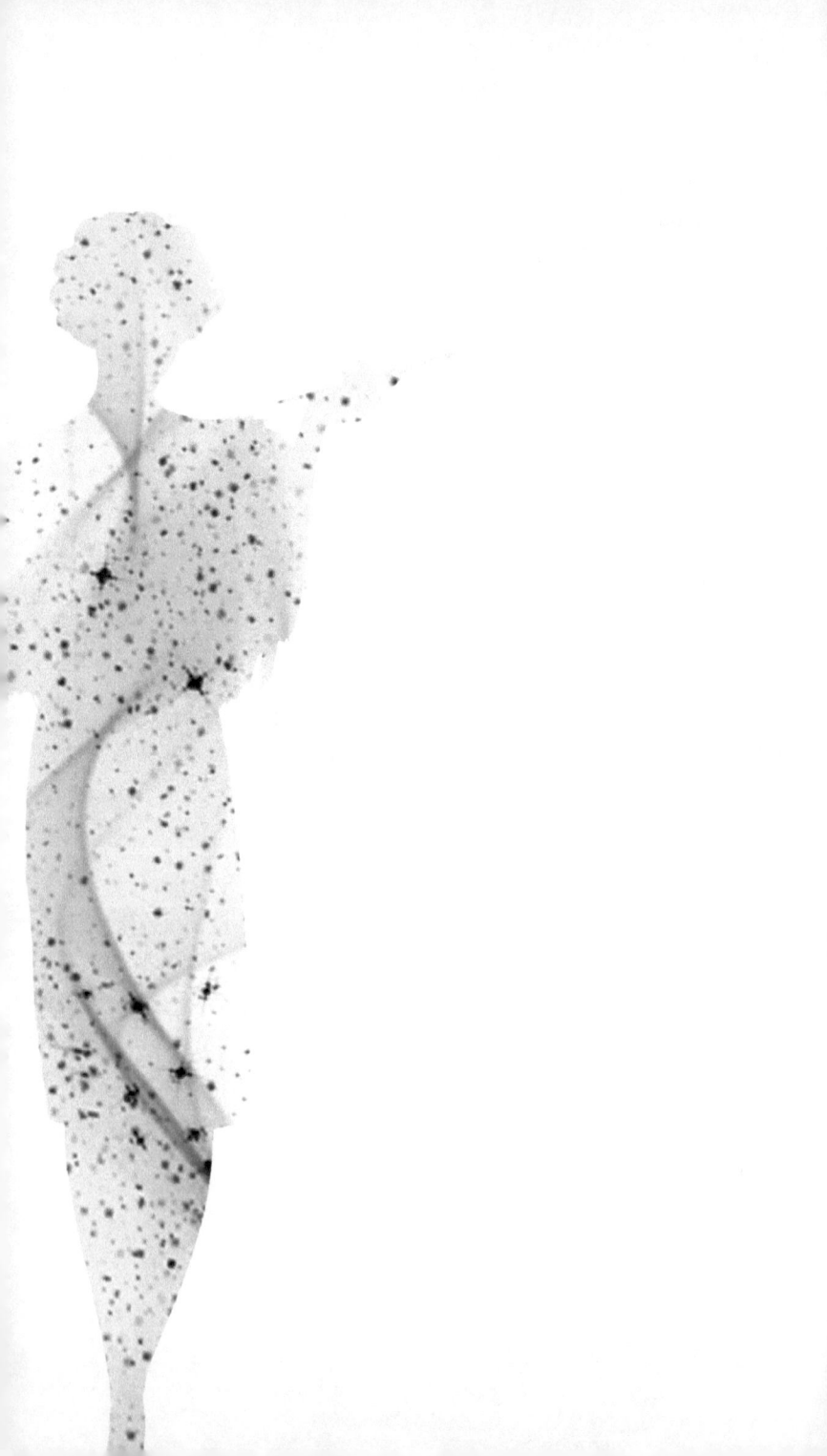

8

Accelerando

THEIR CONVERSATION IS INTERRUPTED BY a phone call. More bad news, though Magdalena can't tell what exactly is going on. Adriano just ushers her back to the bedroom as he takes the call. Even though he has stormed away to the other side of the house, she can hear him raging at the person on the other end of the phone. Muffled shouts of anger echo through the walls. Something's gone wrong at the main dock—vandalism from the sound of it. And cost... the cost for repairs. Expensive by the sound of it. Money. It's always money. That's what got them in this mess in the first place. Money, greed, avarice. It's disgusting.

The front door slams open and shut, Magdalena's husband storming out of the house to put out whatever new fire has sprung up. Put it out with mermaid tears?

Magdalena vacillates. What should she do? What can she do? She doesn't know the first thing about mermaids or tearing or how to be a hero. She isn't built for this kind of thing. Heroes are people from stories. They're the characters she reads about who fight dragons and save villages and rescue damsels in distress. None of them look anything like Magdalena.

She considers calling on Fabien and reporting the situation to him, but what would the technomancer even do? Tearing isn't illegal. Adriano isn't breaking any laws. The only people who might care are ... well, hexen, and she can't go to them. She can't go to Olga. Can she?

Well, it doesn't exactly matter if she can because she has no way to contact the witch.

She still has the hard drive in her pocket. She knows where to go. She could just go herself. She could do the right thing and rescue the mermaid. No, she *should* do the right thing.

So, Magdalena makes her choice. Adriano keeps a laser pistol in a safe in the closet. He bought it not long after they moved into this house, and he made sure Magdalena knew the code in case of an emergency. She always wondered why he'd felt the need to keep a weapon in the house. Now, she knows, and she's thankful for it as she clips the holster to her belt.

Before she can talk herself out of it, she strides to the front door, throws it open, and—

"Olga!"

The woman looks as surprised to see her as Magdalena is surprised to see her. Her hand is raised like one character from a romantic comedy who is about to knock on the door, but then their love interest either walks right out or they chicken out of knocking entirely. In her other hand is Magdalena's grocery sack.

The witch takes one look at Magdalena, sees the weapon at her hip, and holds her hands up in front of her like a banker faced with a robber.

"Look, I realize you probably don't want to see me right now, and I'm sorry about the palm reading thing. I didn't mean to make you feel—"

"Shut up and come with me."

Magdalena closes the door behind her, takes Olga by the hand, and tugs her down the walkway, groceries forgotten on the step.

"Wha—"

"I believe you."

"You do? But your husband—"

"I don't know the specifics, and I don't know if the mermaid you're looking for is still alive, but there's an unregistered ship container in my husband's name. It's not on any of the company records, and I've never heard him mention buying a container. It's also a ways away from the trading pier. Odd, don't you think, for something that is supposed to go on a cargo ship?"

"Wait a minute. Magda, stop. What are you talking about?"

"I went into my husband's study, and I found... I found a hard drive with... with... oh, Olga. It was horrible."

"You found proof that he's been taking mermaids."

"I found more than that. I—I can't believe he would do such a thing."

Olga looks at her pityingly. "He wouldn't be the first human to forge a profit on mermaid tears, and unfortunately, he won't be the last."

Right, well...

Magdalena tugs Olga to her car, a little two-seater parked at the end of the driveway. Olga settles herself in the passenger seat and buckles herself in. As Magdalena starts the engine, the woman shifts with discomfort, her knees pressing together, feet pressed hard into the floor. *Does she not like cars? Maybe she gets motion sickness?*

"You okay?"

"Oh, don't mind me. Go for it."

Maybe she just isn't used to being in a giant box of steel and mechanical engineering.

With that in mind, Magdalena pulls out of the driveway and guides the car through the city traffic carefully. She tries not to think too much on Olga's fingers turning almost translucent; she's gripping the seatbelt so hard. It's a short fifteen-minute drive from her house to the location on the hard drive, and she knows she's in the right place when she parks a ways down the road.

Adriano's SUV is parked right alongside the container.

"He's here."

Olga looks at her and then pulls a small mirror from her coat.

"What are you doing?"

"Calling the boys."

"With a mirror?"

She gives her a crooked smile before tracing a symbol over the glass. Magdalena inhales sharply as the mirror's face begins to glow pink with chaos magic. The woman's reflection disappears, and one of the boys who kidnapped Magdalena appears in its stead.

"We found her," says Olga.

"You found her!"

"Yes. Get down here as quickly as you can. We have company. I'll leave the mirror open. You can use it to navigate."

"We'll be there as quickly as we can."

"Excellent."

Olga puts the mirror facedown at her feet and looks at Magdalena. "Are you sure you want to do this?"

Is she? She's not even really sure what walking into that cargo container will mean for her. She knows the truth already. The truth about her husband, her marriage, her life. So many things built on a lie forged in pain and anguish. But somehow walking into the darkness of it will make it so much more real than if she turned the car back on and drove away.

Olga sets her hand on the center console, not quite touching Magdalena's hand but close enough that her nerves light up.

"The boys and I can handle this ourselves if you want to walk away. No one will blame you. You've already done so much more than I would ever expect of a plusie."

"Plusie?"

"A Human+. That's what you are, right? An augmented human. Someone who is human + technology."

"I've never heard that term before."

"It's a hexen word for people like you. A loving nickname if you will. Cyborg is such a charged word and posthuman is overused."

"People like me."

"People different from us."

"Is difference a bad thing?"

"Only if you make it so."

Magdalena nods. "I need to do this."

Olga sets a hand on Magdalena's shoulder sagely, understanding shining through the angle of her smile. "Then let's do it together."

The car doors shut with a determined click that seems to echo through Magdalena's bones. Olga comes up alongside her as she walks down the sidewalk. Even though summer is fast approaching, Magdalena feels chilled to the bone and the line of her body is warm.

A chain-link fence marks the parameter, and Magdalena stalls Olga before she can step past the gate, hanging ajar on its hinges. "Hold on."

"What is it?"

Magdalena can't see any security systems, but that doesn't mean there aren't any around. "I know my husband. He wouldn't leave something this important to a simple lock and chain."

"Can you hack into a security system?"

"No," she admits sheepishly. "If I can locate them, can't you... I don't know... magic us past them?"

Olga raises an eyebrow at that. "You don't know very much about witches, do you?"

"Can't say I've ever studied the ins and outs of hexen, no. But I've seen some pretty wicked stuff on the news."

"Mhmm, and how often do you hear of witches who can teleport?"

Magdalena winces. "Not very often I guess."

"That's because witches that powerful are rare, gifted with dominion over complex branches of magic. They are exceptional in the same way technomancers are considered exceptional among human+. Most of us are limited by our natural abilities. Some of us are good with herbs and potions, others are exemplary at psychic abilities, and others have a natural inclination toward a certain element. We don't get to choose. It's a roll of the dice made when we are born."

"So, what are your powers?"

Olga pulls aside the sleeve of her blouse to reveal the purplish mark there. Two circles, one surrounding the smaller, and knotted through the smaller circle are four cross sections, the lines cutting through the diameters of the circle. It's her indicia. The mark of her magic.

"This is the aegis knot. I am a shield. My magic is designed to protect and give aid to a person in need. I can make magical shields or force fields, but I'm not one for an offensive disposition, so no, I can't just teleport us past any security cams."

To protect and defend. So unlike what Magdalena knows of witchcraft. The League tribunals always paint witches as fire and brimstone, destruction incarnate, yet here is Olga telling her she can do nothing more than create force fields with her magic.

"So, you can't do anything to help us past the security?"

"Well," Olga scratches her cheek. "I might be able to do something. If you can tell me where they are pointed, I can obstruct the cams long enough for us to get past."

Magdalena blinks. "You can do that?"

"Shields don't need to be see-through, and I can set one pretty much anywhere, so where are the cameras?"

Magdalena pulls out her comm unit. She is not a hacker in any way, shape, or form, but she does know her husband's security codes as well as his preferred security company. He always uses his birthday, and she's told him time and time again that he needs to vary his passcodes. She logs into the security network and inputs Adriano's passcode: 1324AVilla. Unsurprisingly, the network lets her in. She flips through the various cam footage. There are two around the house, a few at his main dock, and a few hooked up to his bigger mining vessels, but she isn't finding a feed that matches their present location—which begs the question: does he really not have this place cammed?

Unlikely. It's bound to be hidden somewhere. She clicks to open up the first cam footage from the house right as a bird flits across the viewer. Opened in full screen, she can swipe through the different feeds. There she finds it, a small icon in the corner of the feed of her backyard, hidden by the atrociously carved hedge towards the back of her insanely expensive pool which she has only used once. She clicks on it and expands to a feed that looks somewhat like their surroundings.

"I think the camera is somewhere to the upper left of the front door."

Olga nods and turns toward the container. The feel of Olga's magic unfolding is indescribable. It's like the taste of the ozone before lightning strikes ... like the way the air on the dance floor thickens right before the bass drops. The smell of a favorite food when you imagine it in your head. Olga's magic unfolds like a blooming flower, and it's no wonder magic is forbidden; just being in the vicinity of this woman weaving a spell is like having morphine injected straight into her bloodstream. She feels giddy and lightheaded all of the sudden, and she floats in the sensation until Olga's hand closes around her own.

"Hey, you ready?"

Magdalena swallows. "Yeah."

The lock on the cargo container hangs off its hinge, and an unfamiliar voice echoes from inside the steel container.

"I already told ya, Adrian. This un's done fer it."

Olga and Magdalena keep their heads low as they peek through the crack in the door. Adriano stands, feet fixed in a wide stance and arms crossed over his chest next to a large burly looking man, the likes of whom Magdalena has never seen before. And before both men, a mermaid—a real live mermaid with a purple-gray fishtail and pure white hair— hangs from a hook: broken, bruised, and dying. The poor thing sits in a half-empty tank of water, tail-up, head-down, and she struggles limply against a position that is surely suffocating her.

The sight is so startling, Olga has to slap a hand over Magdalena's face to keep her from screaming.

"We ain't gotten any tears outta her in days. I sez ya cut her tail off already and throw her back in the dip."

The man is outfitted with a toolbelt, but the accoutrements dangling from the leather are anything but constructive: daggers, pliers, needles, a lighter, instruments of pain.

"No, it could be months before we find another mermaid." Her husband's voice drifts through the venting, tense and angry, the way he'd sounded over the phone. "You get more tears out of this one or find yourself another employer."

"Find myself 'nother employer, eh? Good luck finding sumbody to replace me. I give ya gold everytime without fail. When I sez she done, she done. 'Sides, what ya did with all the pearls I coaxed outta her already? Don't tell me that money gone."

"We've been in the red for months. I needed the money to keep the business going."

"Perhaps ya shoulda thought 'bout that before you accepted that there proposal from Boleria. Lucretia is nothing if not a cutthroat."

"If I had known, I wouldn't have accepted her deal, but you were the one talking about making a profit."

"Well, be that as it may. I ain't workin' her over no more today. You git rid of her and find a different one, or you gonna be out a tearing man."

"Please, Ezekiel. Just one more day with this one. That's all I ask. *Por favor*."

"You want one mo' day, then I want double pay."

"Ezekiel."

"No? Then do her over yerself, ya bastard. I'm done."

"Fine, double pay, provided you get more tears from her tomorrow. No tears and none of us get paid."

Ezekiel clicks his tongue in agreement, hissing something in a language Magdalena can't understand, but he packs up his things to head out, shooting a thumbs up to Adriano.

Magda glances at Olga; the woman looks paler than even her creamy complexion might deem reasonable and more than a little green around the gills. Not that Magdalena can blame her. She herself feels like her lunch is threatening to spill out her mouth and nose, nauseated as she is by ... by everything really. The mermaid, the tearer, his price for inflicting pain, her husband, the lie, the truth...

Gods and Goddesses! The truth, a more horrid thing than Magdalena could have ever imagined. And the ugliest part of it?

Never once did Magdalena question the poisonous fruits they reaped in blood and anguish. In fact, she gladly took a bite, two, three, countless swallows, filling her stomach on the sorrows of others entirely unknowing and unsuspecting.

Now she knows... Ignorance, though passive in nature, is as damning a sin as sloth's six more active counterparts.

9

Sing, Sing, Sing

MAGDALENA REMEMBERS READING AN old-world fairy tale when she was little about a mermaid princess who wanted nothing more than to walk on the shore on her own two feet. She remembers this first version of the story she read had a happy ending. The sea maiden gets her legs, her voice, and her love. It wasn't until she was older that she read the original version of the fairy tale, the one where the human chooses a sea witch instead and the mermaid dissolves into seafoam, her heart broken and her life ruined by a magic spell that was supposed to help her.

Looking now at the rusted tank and the suspended mermaid, gray and sickly from abuse, Magdalena can't help but think the mermaid in the story even more of a fool than the Brothers Grimm wrote her to be.

This is the result of close contact with humans: hung by the tail and tortured for something considered expensive and precious when the reality is, it's just a tear.

Olga has enough sense to tug her around the side of the building before Adriano and Ezekiel barrel right into them.

They trade one last muffled exchange before shaking hands and heading off to their respective vehicles.

Magdalena exhales. She didn't even realize she was holding her breath.

"Come on. We've got to get her out of there before they come back."

"But—"

"Come on, Magda!"

Olga pulls her by the hand from their little hidey hole. The container door is locked, the pull bar bolted into place by a heavy-duty padlock. *Damn!* If it had been a computerized lock, she might have been able to guess Adriano's passcode, but good old-fashioned iron is still as reliable in this day and age as it was two thousand years ago, and if Magdalena knows her husband, (which let's be honest, she's learning very quickly how little she does know him) the key will be in his physical storage system either in his forearm or upper thigh.

"I don't have the key."

Pale pink lips quirk up into a crooked smile. "We don't need one."

Magdalena's brow wrinkles in confusion as the woman takes the heavy-duty iron padlock in hand. "Iron may be great for keeping out the fae-folk and vampyres, but it doesn't work so well on hexen. Keep an eye out for me though; this might take a while."

The witch begins to chant in a strange language, and the air becomes charged like the thickening of ozone before a lightning storm. Like nothing Magdalena has ever heard before, the deep guttural tones intermingled with high-pitched shrills akin to shattering glass make the hair on the back of her neck stand on end. Adrenaline leaks into her systems, her internal alarms going off and telling her now is the time to run and never look back, yet her feet remain dead-locked to the pavement.

With a raspy exhale, Olga pulls a dagger from her hip. Magdalena winces as the woman slices open her palm. Blood oozes from the wound, shimmering eerily with some sort of bioluminescence. She grips the padlock in her bleeding fist, and steam hisses from the metal. She continues the incantation even though her voice wavers and her breathing becomes labored, the words more gasped jumbles than actual spoken text, and then, as though heated to its melting point, the iron of the lock liquifies, gushing around Olga's hand red hot and burning. The smell of melting flesh stings Magdalena's nose.

"What the—! Olga, stop!"

The witch rips her hand away with a shout, and the molten iron drips from her hand in bubbling rivulets, leaving Olga's hand burned by steam and boiling liquid. The battered limb twitches and shakes, exposed sinew and bone smoking like overcooked meat.

"Olga!" Magdalena tries to remember if the better thing to do is wrap a burn with clean cloth or stick it in cold water (*do the same rules apply for molten metal as boiled water?*), but then remembers that she has neither on her person right now. All for nothing though as Olga, wincing from the pain of exposed nerve-endings, pulls a bandage from her bag.

"What did you do?" asks Magdalena as the woman winds the fabric around her gnarled hand.

Olga gives her a grimace that she thinks was supposed to resemble a smile or some sort but falls unbearably short.

"Witch blood with the right invocation can achieve a lot of things, so long as you're willing to pay the price."

A glob of flesh drips from the back of Olga's hand, landing with a wet splatter on the ground.

"And this is an acceptable price?" The inflection behind the words betrays Magdalena's shock and disgust. *How can something so self-destructive ever be acceptable? The woman just mutilated herself to get through a locked door! No wonder the League stresses the abominable-ness of magic. This is how it repays its users—by scarring them for life?*

"Wounds can heal. Death is permanent. A few scars are a small price to pay if it means saving the life of a person people care greatly for."

"But—"

She isn't even human...

The thought comes and goes like a sour-smelling flatulence, an ugly stain in her nostrils that sticks and doesn't go away no matter how much she wants to shake it out. Even though she doesn't voice it to Olga, shame floods her being anyway. How could she think something so vile?

"But what?" asks Olga, opening the door.

"Nothing. Let's just go."

The inside of the warehouse is dark. The halogens are turned off, and the little light that filters in through the doorway and the air-holes lining the container's walls is already dying with the setting sun. The only light in the room is the dull purple glow of the mermaid's fins, and Magdalena's not really sure it can be called a light. It is so faint, weak and blotchy with the angriest glow emanating from the inflamed area around the iron hook.

Olga hurries over to the tank, kneeling in front of the glass. The mermaid barely stirs, her eyelashes fluttering like dying butterflies.

"She doesn't have very long. Your husband's friend was right when he said she was done for."

"That man wasn't any friend of ours."

Olga looks at her oddly before saying, "I guess they weren't exactly cushy, were they?" She tosses her hair the opposite direction and steps for the tank, and Magdalena blushes, realizing the absurdity of her protest, but before she can say anything, Olga makes a pained hissing sound. "Shit, we won't be able to get her to the ocean like this. In this condition, she won't last more than a minute out of the water, even the wretched muck she's currently in."

"I thought mermaids could breathe out of water."

"Under normal circumstances, they can for a short amount of time, but that's only when they are in peak condition. Like this... She'll choke on the air. If we want to get her to the shore, we need to transport her in water."

"Do you think those boys can move the tank?"

"Not without a forklift. Give me a second, and I'll see if I can even get the damned thing open."

Without another word or even glance in Magdalena's direction, Olga walks around to the far side of the tank, leaving Magdalena feeling even more alone than she ever did even on Adriano's latest nights at the rig, or rather where she thought was the rig.

Sweet Xochilt! How many mermaids have been cried to death in this room?

Shaking the thought away, Magdalena wanders over to the side wall where it looks like oodles of equipment have been kept for storage and easy access. There are nets and large fishing hooks, menacing looking electrical harpoons and submarine rifles, a line of various handheld tools—some crude, some of more recent invention—the usage of which Magdalena doesn't want to so much as contemplate, and beside all that is a simple wheelbarrow, large enough for several bags of sand or, she realizes, one tangled up mermaid.

She hurries to test the weight. While it might be a bit on the heavy side, it's in working order and in near perfect condition. Surely those two tidewalkers can push it with their mother inside to the docks.

The tap, tap, tapping of water draws her attention to a leaky pipe protruding from the wall, a long fireman's hose attached to the end. Holding a hand below the leak, she brings a droplet to her lips, and when she finds the water salty, she looks for the end of the hose, a pointed nozzle with a pull lever for pressure control. Unthinking, she tugs the handle all the way to the end, releasing a powerful gush of water. It hits the wall with a deafening spray that rebounds to soak her clothing before she manages to wrestle the lever to a lower setting. A much more manageable slosh of perfectly fresh saltwater cascades down to puddle at her feet.

It must be linked to the sea or at least an underground lagoon. *Perfect!*

"Olga," she calls, rushing back to the tank. "I found a working seawater valve and a wheelbarrow. We can fill it with water and get her back to the ocean this wa—" Magdalena draws up short at the sight that meets her back at the tank.

"Get the fuck up."

Adriano's pistol is buried in Olga's hair. When the witch doesn't move fast enough, a shudder coursing from the top of her head to her boots, Adriano lifts the weapon skyward and pulls the trigger. Magdalena flinches at the deafening bang, rooftop debris falling over her head and shoulders in dusty crumbles.

"I said get up!"

He presses the gun's nozzle back against Olga's scalp. The smell of burning hair makes Magdalena gag as the blonde rises to her feet.

"Good. Hands where I can see them."

"Alright, alright. Don't shoot. I'm not armed."

"The hell you're not, witch. Taking advantage of my sick wife so you can use her against me. You think I'm a fool?"

"I haven't done anything to her—"

"Shut up! You spew another word, and we'll see how bulletproof witches are, after all."

"Adriano, sweetheart, please." Magdalena's voice cracks on the word "sweetheart." "Why don't you put down the gun? I'm not under a spell. Olga hasn't done anything to—"

"Hush, Magda. You're confused and vulnerable. She's obviously been taking advantage of the fact that you're a Wúxíng patient. Just stay there, and I'll take care of this *perra* one way or another, and we'll get the dispel corps to relieve you of whatever enchantment has you doing something as stupid as working with a hexen."

SING, SING, SING

"Adriano," she calls, firmer. "How could you do something like this? For money! Let the mermaid go."

"I said stop talking, Magda!"

"Don't yell at her!"

"I said shut up, witch!"

Adriano strikes Olga across the back of the head. The witch tumbles forward into the mermaid's tank unconscious; blood bubbles from the wound, coloring the water.

"Olga!"

In the tank, the mermaid rouses, webbed hands coming up to shake Olga awake to no avail. Only before she can get a good grip on the witch, Adriano pulls a nearby lever, and the chain connected to the hook embedded in the fae's tail rapidly recoils, pulling the creature out of the water. Within moments, the shrillest sound Magdalena has ever heard spills from the mermaid's mouth. The water of the tank churns angrily and the metal walls of the container shake, but it ends as quickly as it began as the mermaid begins to choke on the dry air.

"Adriano, stop it! You're going to kill them!"

"So what!" he snaps, waving the pistol in the air. "They aren't human anyway."

Magdalena recoils as though slapped as Adriano gives voice to the very same thought that skirted across her consciousness only moments ago.

"They're people, Adriano." She hates how her voice trembles as though she isn't so sure of the words herself. "They're people!" she repeats, firmer.

Adriano just scoffs. "They're monsters, Magda. No more than that."

Monsters? How can a mermaid who cares enough to love her hexen children despite the barriers of land and sea be considered a monster?

Olga, who saved her life... Olga, who kept her company on a lonely night... Olga, the witch who helped her uncover the truth about the bloodstained life she's been living...

Olga, a monster?! Why? Because she's a witch? That is sup-posed to make her a monster by default!

"No, they aren't!" She sets her stand, voice rising by the decibel.

"Magda," Adriano chides.

"No! If there's a monster in this room, it's you!"

Her husband looks at her like a man betrayed.

"Magda, mi amor, I did all of this for you. I've done all of this to make sure you are taken care of."

"You say you did all of this for me. Well, guess what? You've lost me. You think I want to be married to a man who made his fortune by causing pain and suffering? You're not the man I married, and I will not let you take another life for the sake of your petty greed."

"That's the damned magic talking. You don't know what you're saying."

"I know exactly what I'm saying."

"Do you now? Because you seem to have forgotten what happened to your grandmother because she was delusional enough to believe magic could help her. Just another type of witch, if you ask me, and she got what she deserved in the end—a horrible, painful death, all alone because the government no longer saw her fit enough to take care of a small child."

Her grandmother hadn't been a witch, but rather than getting augmented or enduring all sorts of medical proce-dures like Magdalena had during her teens, she kept her own little rituals, collecting shells, tracing protection charms in the sand, and leaving small offerings for the local fae-folk and spirits at different points in the year. Magdalena always wondered about it. Maybe that was why it took so long for her to succumb to the ailment, the small practices keeping the surplus energy at bay even if her abuelita couldn't actively manipulate the magic inside her.

However, because of this, the superstitious and unin-formed used to think her grandmother a witch, but the truth of it is that if her grandma had been a witch, the ailment wouldn't have killed her. She wouldn't even have gotten it. That was why the local doctors refused to help her toward the end. That was why the local government took her away from her grandmother when she most needed her, sending her to live with a distant relative in the city.

Maybe that's why Magdalena decided to go into education. Perhaps in some small way she could help stop the spread of ignorance that resulted in her grandmother's death.

"How dare you! My grandmother died a horrible death, yes, but it wasn't one she brought on herself."

"She refused medical help, she failed to listen to the doctors, and she condemned you to the same ailment because of it. Don't be a fool to make the same mistake."

Inside the tank, Olga thrashes, bubbles spewing out of her mouth as she inhales a lungful of salt water.

"I'll show you a mistake."

And Magdalena pulls the lever on the hose. A jet of water explodes from the nozzle, hitting Adriano square in the chest. He flails back at the impact, tumbling into the wall. The mermaid falls back into the tank, water splashing onto the platform. Adriano's feet fling out from under him, and he slides, face-first, into the water. He latches onto Olga, who tries to swim her way back out of the tank, but the mermaid yanks on the man's upper body, dragging him to the bottom as Magdalena's witch sputters her way to the surface.

Magdalena looks on in horror as the tank floods with bubbles, Adriano's face twisted with panic as the mermaid steals his remaining breath with a scornful kiss. It is Olga who coaxes her to turn away as her husband's struggles weaken and die, and where she expects to feel horror, she, instead, feels numb with relief.

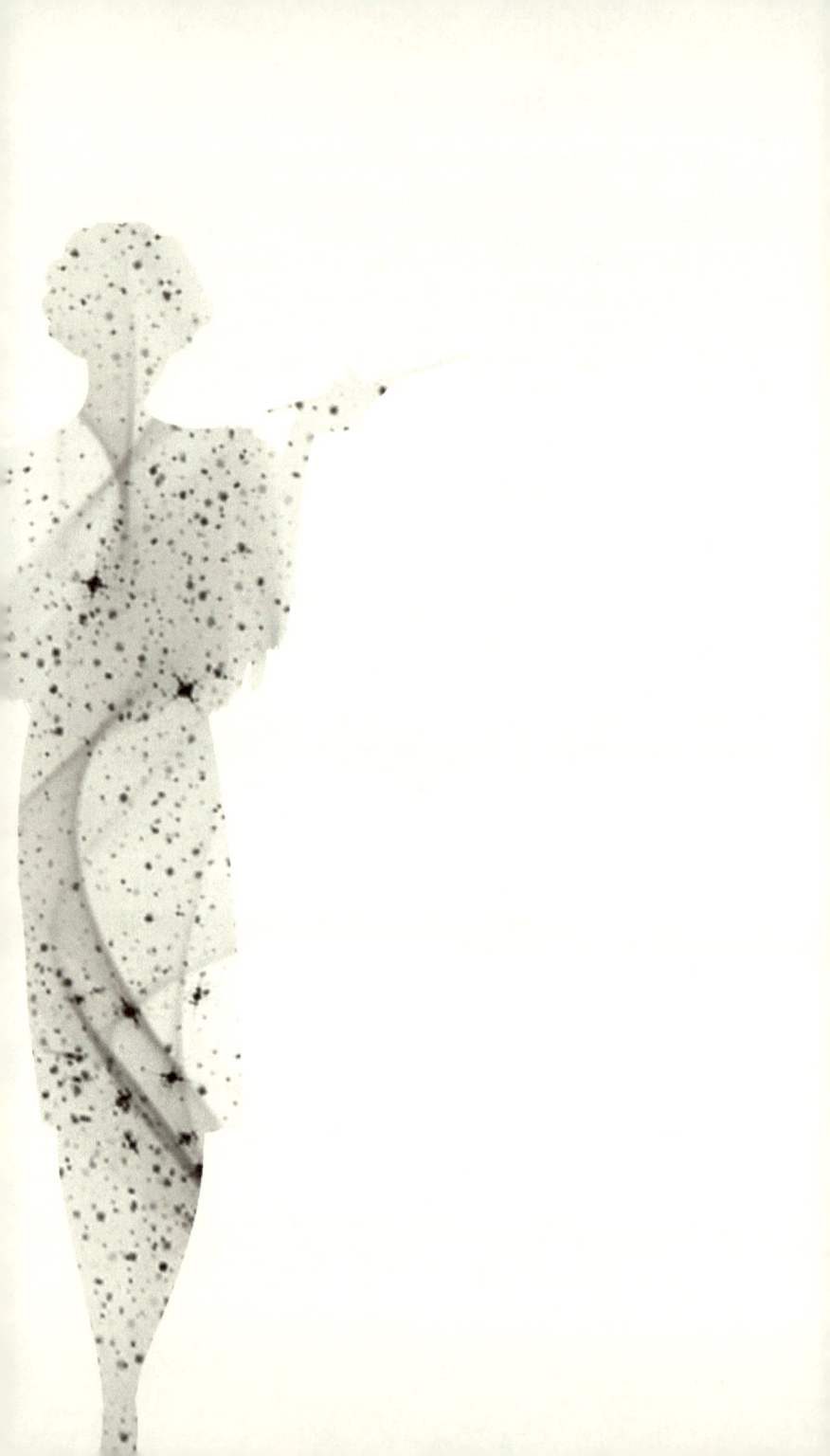

10

Resonance

MAGDALENA AND OLGA WATCH FROM A distance as the two boys lower their mother into the water. She can see the relief that alights on the mermaid face as the saltwater folds around her for the first time in who knows how long.

Standing on the dock as the three disappear, Magdalena fights back tears. The notes of the siren's song folding and unfolding around her like a hymn to the sea, couched by the breaking of the waves on the pier.

"I've lost everything."

Olga looks at her.

"I can't ever go back to my life. Not with Adriano dead. Not with me being the reason he's gone."

"That man would have killed you as readily as he would have killed me. He didn't see you as a person, Lena. He saw you as a trophy."

"I know that, but he was my husband." Years of her life spent with someone, and what does she have to show for it? A broken heart. Lies. A numbness so final she wonders if she is ever going to have the ability to feel again. "What am I going to do?"

Olga tucks her fingertips under Magdalena's chin.

"You have enchanted me beyond any magic spell or bewitchment. I can't tell you what to do. I can't tell you where to go. I can't even begin to understand the pain and confusion and betrayal you might be feeling knowing that someone you love took part in something so horrible. What I can tell you is that I will not let you handle this alone. I won't tell you to run away with me, but there are places you can go where you can be safe, and I can help you get to them. If you need a friend, a family, a confidante, I am here for you. If you need more than that, I am here for you. If you need less, I can give that, too. It's your call, Magdalena. I owe you much for the sacrifice you have made for a creature that until just days ago you thought was just another monster."

Olga's hair looks like liquid fire in the light of the setting sun, and her eyes take on this orangy tint, blue gold waiting to be melted into something far more beautiful and far more valuable than a teardrop pearl shed in pain and agony, and it steals Magdalena's breath away when she realizes that that priceless piece of finery is being offered to her.

"You don't owe me anything, Olga."

"Perhaps not, but if I hadn't come along, you'd be living your life as usual."

"I would be living a lie. Better to lose everything than living in a house of mirrors and illusions."

Olga chews on her lower lip, shifting her weight from one foot to the other.

"Perhaps not everything, Magdalena." Magdalena looks at the woman next to her in confusion. Olga's eyes sparkle like the palest of sapphires in the moonlight. "Once we're away from here, I think you should take a pregnancy test."

"What?"

"Call it a witch's intuition, but I think you're pregnant, Lena."

Magdalena's hands fly to her stomach. Shock, happiness, and just a touch of terror ripple from her toes to her head. Could it be true? Is she pregnant? After so many years of trying, is she finally going to get the family she has always wanted?

She looks back up at Olga, eyes glittering with unshed tears. "I'm—I'm pregnant?"

Olga smiles.

"I saw it in your palm, and I see it now in your aura, two differing colors, and even if the second is but a tiny flame, it is there and growing ever stronger."

The tears spill over, her heart overflowing, yet she does not turn from Olga's gaze. There is comfort in those eyes, and the same connection she felt instantaneously with the woman hovers suspended in time between them, and Magdalena can't look away.

"Will you be there with me when—when I take the test?"

Golden blond lashes blink in surprise. "So long as you want me there."

"I do want you there, Olga," says Magdalena, leaning forward. Because in such a short time, the witch has already given her the greatest gift anyone could ever give her.

Olga's lips feel like a boundless truth.

Epilogue

7 Months Later–2nd Day in the Month of Hearths, 1854 A.P–City of Lorelei

MAGDALENA DECORATES HER FIRST Yule tree under Olga's careful scrutiny. Not because the witch doesn't trust her to do it correctly but because Magdalena's belly has been making movement terribly difficult for about two months now. She is prohibited from getting up on the step stool, her ability to bend over has been severely compromised, and let's just say her balance is a bit off, but she is determined to decorate this tree, the first marker of their new home that will be wholly theirs and not something scavenged from a back alley or borrowed from one of their new neighbors. The lycan family is kind enough, but Magdalena is still rather uncomfortable knowing the vast majority of their decor is from animals they killed themselves, and the howling at the full moon last month scared her out of her wits.

"You realize I haven't put up a Yule tree since I was a teenager, right?" Olga's voice is light and breathy with laughter as she hands Magdalena a bright red ornament.

"Yes, you keep saying so, but it's part of your culture, and I want to celebrate it. Besides, once Lucy is born, we'll have to get in the habit of celebrating the holidays properly."

"I know, I know, but I keep flinching every time your bump brushes against the branches."

Magdalena chuckles. The little orb sparkles in the fire-light while the old box radio she found in an antique shop plays through a staticky jazz rendition of "Stille Nacht."

"It's not like they can hurt me."

"I know, but it's just another thing for you to maneuver around, and you can't exactly see your feet these days."

"It's fine," she coos, reaching up on her tippy toes to hang the ornament from a higher branch.

The radio frequency spikes, the music cutting off with a sour bend to the note.

"We interrupt this broadcast with breaking news from Deriva's capital. After months of pressure from citizens, the Vulcan has announced a culling of oceanic fae, monsters, and hexen off the coasts of Deriva. This comes in the wake of the untimely death of his majesty's second wife, the Firefly Freya Nocturne, who was dragged out to sea in her efforts to save both the crown prince and her daughter from a sea dragon. Prince Xipilli is unharmed, and the young Lady Wren Nocturne is in recovery after suffering several serious injuries. While our hearts go out to Vulcan Tlanextli and his family in their time of grief, many groups are calling this tragedy a karmic interference as a result of the Vulcan's inaction to address civilian concerns after a local sea miner was found drowned in what appeared to be a mermaid attack. Adriano Villanueva's wife is still missing, and we can only hope justice can be served for both the Villanueva couple and our Vulcan's late concubine."

The blood drains from Magdalena's bones, and Olga has to catch her by the waist to guide her into a chair before she can fall to the ground. *Is this what a centuries-long war looks like?*

"Goddess above... Freya... that little girl... Oh gods, how many people are going to die because of what I did?"

"Magda, shh, shh. This is not your fault."

"But—"

"It's not your fault," Olga hushes, firmly in her ear. Her arms wind tight around Magdalena's midsection, the decorations forgotten as the witch rocks her back and forth, back and forth, gently, like the rolling waves of the ocean under a ship, and though Magdalena mourns—for a woman she only met once and for the countless lives about to be lost in the resurging of an age-old feud—Olga's love cradles her the way the sea cradles the land.

Love, whether newly born or aroused from a death-like slumber, must always create sunshine, filling the heart so full of radiance, that it overflows upon the outward world.

The Scarlet Letter
Nathaniel Hawthorne, 1850 A.D.

Glossary of Terms

- Adept – An augmented person equipped with military–grade technology. Certified to hunt and track hexen.
- Deriva – An island country within the League, Deriva is home to a constitutional monarchy led by the Vulcan.
- Cyborg – An augmented person possessing a set minimum of technological enhancements, or a human+ possessing enhancements essential to their ability to live (i.e. respiratory life support, mechanical hearts, spinal augmentations to prevent paralysis).
- Fae – Fairy Folk – Magical creatures that pre–date witchcraft in Deus. The Fae generate their own wild magic and live independently of witches. (Examples of Fae in Deus: Pixies, Nymphs, Mermaids, Trolls)
- Hexen – The Spell Folk – Magic users and creatures reliant or resultant of witchcraft. (Examples of Hexen: Witches, Werewolves, Vampyres, Goblins)
- Human+ – A person who accepted technology into their existence via a permanent integration. This can be as mediocre an augmentation as a cochlear implant or as extensive as a prosthetic limb or neural net.

- Mermaids – Also known as sirens, mermaids and/or merfolk lived in the depths of the Pacificum long before humans arrived in Deus. They are capable of controlling other sea creatures, calling storms, and singing hypnotic ballads that can lure even the most immoveable of sailors to their deaths.
- Palmistry – Also known as chiromancy, palmistry is the practice of telling someone's future by "reading" the lines of their palm. Thought to originate in India, palmistry is suspected to have spread around the world via the Roma as they traveled through China, the Middle East, Mesopotamia, Greece, and eventually Europe. It is now widely practiced around the world in a variety of cultures.
- Technomancer – A League–certified human+ capable of channeling energy through their technology. Technomancers are specially trained and equipped to hunt and kill dangerous fae, hexen, undead, and other magical creatures. Their augmentations are top-of-the-line and require an immense amount of discipline to maintain and control.
- Tidewalker–The half-human/half-merfolk children of mermaids and humans. Tidewalkers inherit a variety of traits from the sea-fae mothers including breathing underwater, siren-song, and some can even manifest fins and gills when submerged in sea water.
- Witch – A practitioner of witchcraft, the act of molding and utilizing wild magic to effect change in the outer world. Witches in Deus achieve their powers and abilities through a mixture of blood–inheritance and practical study and are considered the most dangerous of beings as the practice of unrestricted magics can lead to psychological breakdown and magic fever.

About the Author

LYRA R. SAENZ IS A WRITER OF SCIENCE fiction/fantasy. A romantic at heart with a love for supernatural horror, she believes that while happy endings don't come easily, they do come, even if it means excising your ex into a glass jar.

Born and raised in South Texas, Lyra is a multicultural, eyeliner–wielding member of the LGBTQ+ community, an animal–lover, and a cynic of all things political. She presently haunts the Houston area with her amazingly supportive partner and her feline–shaped void, Violet. Lyra grew up bouncing between her Chicano and Scandinavian heritages never feeling like she really fit in one world or the other.

Despite growing up on enchiladas and lefsa, she'll never turn down an offering of sushi or pho. And while her friends were getting boyfriends and girlfriends, she was too busy crushing on dreamy anime and manhwa characters to bother with real people. So, with one foot on either side of the border and her head full of East–Asian pop culture, she started creating her own worlds.

A lover of all things witchy, paranormal, and ghostly with a side of Victorian–futurism, cyberpunk, and post-humanism, Lyra imagines worlds where the IT tech is a werewolf, and the coffee machine has a fairy living inside it, but the androids love to take walks down the forest trail and host the occasional bonfire. When she isn't lost some-where between an inkwell and a notebook, she can be found acting as a throne for the real queen of the household: her cat, and her royal majesty demands snuggles constantly. Or on calmer days, she'll sit and listen to her partner play video games while she unsuccessfully knits and/or binges her latest international tv show.

https://www.bookwitchsaenz.com/

Facebook: BookWitch.Saenz

Twitter: BookWitch_Saenz

Instagram: BookWitch_Saenz

BookWitchSaenz@gmail.com

More Books...

Prelude

Falsetto in the Woods

Ragtime Swing

Sonata

Song of the Sea

The Devil's Trill

Bercuese

To Heal a Songbird

Ghost March

Nocturne

4 Horsemen Publications
Romance

Ann Shepphird

The War Council

Emily Bunney

All or Nothing
All the Way
All Night Long
All She Needs
Having it All
All at Once
All Together
All for Her

Lynn Chantale

The Baker's Touch
Blind Secrets

Mimi Francis

Private Lives
Second Chances
Run Away Home
The Professor

Fantasy & Paranormal Romance

Beau Lake

The Beast Beside Me
The Beast Within Me
The Beast After Me
The Beast Like Me
An Eye for Emeralds
Swimming in Sapphires
Pining for Pearls

D. Lambert

To Walk into the Sands
Rydan
Northlander
Esparan
King
Traitor
His Last Name

J.M. Paquette

Klauden's Ring
Solyn's Body
The Inbetween
Hannah's Heart
Call Me Forth
Invite Me In

Valerie Willis

Cedric: The Demonic Knight
Romasanta: Father of Werewolves
The Oracle: Keeper of the
Gaea's Gate
Artemis: Eye of Gaea
King Incubus: A New Reign

V.C. Willis

Prince's Priest
Priest's Assassin

Cozy Mysteries

Ann Shepphird

Destination: Maui
Destination: Monterey

Horror, Thriller, & Suspense

Erika Lance

Jimmy
Illusions of Happiness
No Place for Happiness
I Hunt You

Young Adult Fantasy

Blaise Ramsay

Through The Black Mirror
The City of Nightmares
The Astral Tower
The Lost Book of the Old Blood
Shadow of the Dark Witch
Chamber of the Dead God

C.R. Rice

Denial
Anger
Bargaining
Depression
Acceptance
Broken Beginnings:
Story of Thane
Shattered Start: Story of Sera
Sins of The Father: Story of Silas
Honorable Darkness: Story of
Hex and Snip
A Love Lost: Story of Radnar

4HorsemenPublications.com

www.ingramcontent.com/pod-product-compliance
Lightning Source LLC
Chambersburg PA
CBHW050422110726
47899CB00008B/2820